Secrets of Clan Cameron

Three siblings, three secrets to unearth...

Royce leads Clan Cameron with honor, respect and integrity. But he's never wanted to burden anyone else with the responsibility, so the guarded laird often goes it alone.

Susanna Cameron has no trouble speaking her mind. And when she sets her sights on something, there's nothing that will stop her.

Rolf Cameron is a warrior. He fights for what's right. But fighting for what he wants could be a different matter...

The siblings are all about to uncover secrets that have been hidden, not just from them but from their entire clan... Will their determination to discover the truth lead them to change their philosophies on life, leadership...and love?

Read Royce and Iona's story in
A Laird without a Past
Available now!

Look out for Susanna's and Rolf's stories
Coming soon!

Author Note

A Laird without a Past touches on many aspects
of the unseen. Those things we literally cannot see
as well as the secrets we wish to hide, even from
ourselves, and how we maneuver around them
until we are forced to face them head-on. This book
was difficult to write, and I found myself waiting
impatiently for Royce and Iona to share their story
with me so that I could then put it on paper to share
with you. It wasn't until I finished the first draft that
I realized it was I who was resisting their stories,
as part of their journey reflected my own, which
is often the case with my books.

It took me many years to face my own secrets
and to address how they were devouring me from
within. As with all difficult things, once shared they
become less and less powerful, and eventually they
become nothing more than fallen petals carried
away in the wind.

I wish the same peace for you, and I hope you
enjoy Royce and Iona's story.

JEANINE ENGLERT

—

A Laird without a Past

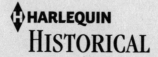

HARLEQUIN
HISTORICAL

HARLEQUIN®
HISTORICAL™

PLEASE RECYCLE
THIS PRODUCT IS RECYCLABLE

Recycling programs for this product may not exist in your area.

ISBN-13: 978-1-335-59561-4

A Laird without a Past

Harlequin Enterprises ULC
22 Adelaide St. West, 41st Floor
Toronto, Ontario M5H 4E3, Canada
www.Harlequin.com

Printed in U.S.A.

Jeanine Englert's love affair with mysteries and romance began with Nancy Drew and her grandmother's bookshelves of romance novels. When she isn't wrangling with her characters, she can be found trying to convince her husband to watch her latest *Masterpiece* or BBC show obsession. She loves to talk about writing, her beloved rescue pups, and mystery and romance novels with readers. Visit her website at www.jeaninewrites.com.

Books by Jeanine Englert

Harlequin Historical

The Highlander's Secret Son

Secrets of Clan Cameron

A Laird without a Past

Falling for a Stewart

Eloping with the Laird
The Lost Laird from Her Past
Conveniently Wed to the Laird

Visit the Author Profile page
at Harlequin.com for more titles.

To the people and community
of Lismore, Scotland,

Thank you for allowing me glimpses of your
beautiful isle. I have fallen in love with a place
I have never been but hope to visit one day.

To my dear readers,

If you would like to help be a part of saving the
gorgeous medieval cathedral church of St. Moluag
on the Isle of Lismore, please visit the website
isleoflismore.com/island-groups/parish-church and
donate. Any and every amount makes a difference.

Thank you in advance for your generosity.

Prologue

The waters of Loch Linnhe, Lismore, Scotland—
August 1745

'I dinna believe they aim to meet us, my laird.'

'Keep rowing, Athol,' Laird Royce Cameron commanded. His gaze searched the moonlit horizon as their oars cut through the shimmering obsidian waters of Loch Linnhe, their small boat gliding towards what he hoped would be the answers he'd long sought.

'They will be here,' Royce added.

He'd not allow himself to believe otherwise. He was weary, bone weary, of the need to discover what had happened to his youngest sister all those years ago that day at sea and why it had taken almost two decades for her to return to their family. This man, Webster, was Royce's last hope.

A faint sluicing of oars through water sounded in the distance and Royce almost sighed aloud when he saw the profile of a boat with two shadowy figures rowing towards them. His heart picked up speed, his urgency to know the truth outweighing everything else.

'Forward,' he ordered.

'Aye,' Athol answered, meeting Royce's gaze. Moonlight reflected off the whites of the man's eyes. Fear rested there and a sliver of doubt slithered along Royce's spine. His fingers tingled as he gripped the smoothed wood of the oar. Athol was one of Royce's most trusted soldiers, his instincts strong and true, his discretion and loyalty to Royce and the Camerons even stronger.

It was one of the many reasons Royce had chosen him for this secret mission to the small and remote isle of Lismore. He alone knew Royce was here to meet with Webster, a man referenced repeatedly in the worn pages of Royce's father's private journals, and in the clan's old financial ledgers, in relation to his youngest sister's disappearance. Not even Royce's siblings knew of his whereabouts and this perilous undertaking and he planned to keep it that way.

If their father was involved in the disappearance of his sister as he'd indicated in his journals, Royce wanted that knowledge to die with him and him alone. Such a grief didn't need to be shared, especially by the people he loved most in this world, his brother and two sisters.

Athol's gaze scanned the horizon from one side to the other with the vigilance of a soldier on the battle-field despite being at sea.

'You do not trust this?' Royce asked, dropping his voice.

Athol's silence was his answer.

Royce ignored it. He'd not give up now when they were so close to the truth. His guilt over his part in losing his sister to the sea when he was a boy had long tormented him. If discovering the truth could heal that wound for him and his siblings, he would chase it to the ends of this earth. He dug his oars and his doubt deep into the waters of the loch and leaned back. They propelled themselves along through the water.

Soon, their boat sidled up alongside the other small vessel and Athol gripped the hull of the other boat with one hand, while his other rested atop the hilt of the dagger in his waist belt. Royce studied the two men and frowned, knowing they were far too young and green to be the man he sought. Webster had known Royce's father almost twenty years ago. These men looked like young soldiers he often trained, their faces still full and unblemished.

'Where is Webster?' Royce demanded, his tone harsh and unyielding. Impatience ate at him. He needed to know the truth. There had to be an end to this agony of not knowing, this guilt of what unforeseen role he had played in his sister's suffering.

'We will deliver you to the meeting location.'

'Bloody hell. That is *not* what was agreed upon,' Royce argued. '*Webster* was to meet us here. Not his lemmings.' He set a glare upon them and scowled.

The youngest of the men reached for his blade. Athol answered the threat in kind by whipping his dagger from its sheath before the lad had removed his own, the metal glinting in the moonlight.

'Careful. Athol cuts first and asks questions later,' Royce warned.

The older of the two scowled. 'Do ye wish to see Webster or not?'

'Aye.'

'Then follow us to the main ship. 'Tis easier to have the conversation ye seek there. But yer dog stays here.'

'Nay,' Athol answered, extending his blade and lunging forward. 'They are not to be trusted. I can smell their deceit.'

Royce gripped his friend's forearm. It was too late to turn back. This was his only chance for the truth. 'I will go. Await here. I will return within the hour.'

Athol's fierce gaze showed his displeasure, but he obeyed the order and allowed Royce to pass.

He stepped aboard the small skipper and turned back to Athol, who nodded to him. If Royce did not return within the hour, Athol would rip the island to shreds in search of him. Such a knowing put Royce at ease. As he settled into the boat, he glanced over and saw a man rising from the waters like a mystical creature behind Athol. Before Royce could shout a warning, the man slit Athol's throat.

'No!' Royce cried out and strained against the two men struggling to hold him back. Athol gripped his throat, the blood seeping through his fingers, his eyes wide with shock and anger.

'Hit 'im!' one man shouted as Royce freed one arm and landed several blows to the other man's gut. Finally gaining his freedom, Royce grabbed for the boat's hull, preparing to jump into the waters to reach Athol. It didn't matter if it was too late or not. The man was his friend and soldier. But as Royce's fingertips skimmed the cool waters, the hilt of a sword cracked into his head. The world faded to black.

Chapter One

Iona MacKenzie rolled on to her back to float and the cool water lapped soothingly against her bare skin. The stars dotted the clear midnight sky, and she revelled in the peace the water always gave to her weary body and soul. Here and only here, she felt free…of everything. There was no sound, no heaviness to her limbs, and for a few minutes she could forget who she was and the meagre life she lived.

And pretend she was not alone.

She could close her eyes and imagine herself as someone else, even if only for a few minutes. Tonight, she would be a young wife and mother with a family huddled up in a small cottage in town listening to the sound of her children playing with one another while her husband read aloud from a book by the warm, flickering fire. She breathed deeply. The smell of the evening stew still lingered in the air and the stars glistened outside their window as she darned a stocking and smiled upon the scene before her.

The story played out smoothly in her mind and

she smiled at the imaginary world she had created. It mirrored her childhood before her world had been turned on end.

Her chest tightened at the memory of the happy life she had once had with her parents in the small herbal store and the even tinier rooms they had lived in above it before her mother had died when she was seven and then her father a decade later.

Iona dared not risk the idea of having a family again. It was far safer to remain alone. Loss had almost eaten her alive more than once. She'd not let grief gain another grip upon her now. Her solitary life as a reclusive healer was a product of her own creation after she'd lost her parents and it served her well, providing her the life of independence and control she craved.

Iona clung to the predictable quiet her own company brought and scarcely emerged from it. She lived far away from anyone on the isle in her father's old cottage on the shore surrounded by the animals she had healed and her best friend, a hound named Jack. She had everything she needed and she would be wise to remember such.

'Fool,' she muttered, splashing the water with her hand. She had no business wishing for anything more. Hopes and dreams had a way of letting one down.

Such wool-gathering was as dangerous as a rip tide: you couldn't see how it was leading you astray until it pulled you under and dragged you out to sea.

A shout cut through her thoughts, pulling her back to the present.

'Sailor's fortune,' she cursed, opening her eyes and turning towards the noise. She treaded water and watched a group of men stumbling along the pebbled shores of Loch Linnhe. No one was ever out this late, one of the many reasons she completed her daily swim well after dark and away from the prying eyes of the villagers. She frowned. Even from this distance she could deduce the men were far too deep in their cups to be up to anything but mischief…or worse. She'd have to wait them out to return to her cottage unnoticed.

The full moon shone brightly in the dark sky, allowing her to see their staggering shadowy forms and hear their muffled voices as they passed the small cottages and homes dotting the shoreline of Lismore. Soon, they would be on their way to The Laughing Goat Inn nestled at the other end of the beach at the edge of town. Although it wasn't unusual for men to traverse along this way as a throughway from one inn to another, they were usually earlier in the eve in their travels and a touch faster.

She stretched her arms in and out like a bird spreading its wings preparing for flight, propelling herself through the loch. She turned back over and swam for a few strokes before treading water again and glancing back to the shoreline. The men were still there, but why? What were they doing? Two of them were hunched over something on the beach, while the other two men watched.

Her pulse increased. Something was amiss. Was it a wounded animal on the shore? Or a person? Curiosity surpassed her fear of discovery and she increased the speed of her strokes. Her limbs sliced through the water until she was finally able to hear the men clearly. She made certain to remain far enough from shore to be hidden from sight. Drunk men were as dangerous as rabid dogs.

'Just take it all. He doesna' need it now,' one man said and then cackled aloud.

'Check the pockets,' the largest of the men ordered. 'I'll lift 'im.'

Iona baulked. There was a man on the shoreline lying on the sand and rocks, half tangled in sea netting. They were rifling through his pockets. She swallowed hard. The man must be dead.

'Stop!' she called.

When they turned to her, she realised her error. What if *they* had killed him? She should have had a plan in mind *before* she'd revealed herself, but she'd acted on instinct to protect the poor man. She swam faster until she stumbled up the shoreline, her bare feet struggling to grip the sand and pebbles beneath. 'Leave him!' she shouted.

They gaped at her. She knew she wasn't decent. Most likely the sight of her was obscene with her thin, soaked shift clinging to her flesh and hiding little if any of her form, but she didn't care. She was no respectable lady and never would be, and this man who lay still and lifeless in the sand mattered far more than mere propriety.

The sight of the poor man was a brutal reminder of her father and how she'd found him, face down on the shoreline days after the boating accident that had killed him and changed her life for ever. No one deserved to die that way or be pillaged about like they were rubbish. Not her father and not this man either.

His dark wet hair covered much of his face like kelp, his still-open hands clutching the sand as if he had struggled ashore with his last breath. Her heart thundered in her ears and her chest heaved from the exertion. Gooseflesh rose on her skin as the cool air hit her body.

'Glory,' the largest man jeered and whistled. 'Seems a sea nymph has arrived just in time, lads.' His eyes roved over every inch of her and her cheeks heated at the implication and overt lust in his gaze. 'I think I'd like a turn first,' he called, grabbing at his trews, his intent clear and menacing. Fear licked along her skin, but she steeled her spine. It was far too late for anything else.

'Leave him alone,' she said again, louder this time, as another man with a pronounced limp yanked a ring from the dead man's finger.

'Ye gonna stop me, are ye? He has no need fer 'is fancy signet ring now, does he?' he scoffed and shoved the ring in his pocket, letting the man's arm fall lifeless back into the sand.

The band of moonlight was but steps away. All she had to do was step into it, but her stomach made a sickening turn. She knew what would follow.

Do what is right and you will never be alone, my little fish. Her father's words echoed in her ears. She stepped into the moonlight.

'Saints be,' the man who'd ogled her spat out.

'It be the Seafarer's Daughter, the Witch of the Loch,' the largest man murmured, taking a step back.

Iona fought the urge to roll her eyes. The men were dolts.

The man with a limp chimed in. 'Aye,' he said, pointing to her scarred cheek. 'My pa says the sea did that to her. Punishment for all her witchcraft.'

'Nay. She be a healer. Not a witch,' the youngest one attempted to whisper, even though it came out as a slurred shout.

'Aye,' she answered, trying to look as terrifying as she could with her soaked shift and wet, tangled black hair draping down her face and back. 'Are you lads in need of healing?' she mocked, opening her arms and meeting the man's gaze with a wicked smile.

'Nay. Let us go, boys,' he said. 'Ye can have him, witch.'

'Go!' she shouted. 'Before I change my mind.' She lunged at them and they sprinted off, kicking up sand in their wake.

'Drunkards,' she grumbled.

She lifted her shift and rushed ashore. While she was no witch, she had long since given up dispelling any of the rumours surrounding her and her family and their self-imposed isolation. When her mother passed, her father had closed their shop and moved them from town to a remote cottage by the shore, a place to grieve in solitude for a few months and find peace as he coped with her death.

Then, those few months had turned into years,

tripping along one after another, and they had never moved back into town. Solitude became a friend to Iona, especially after Catriona, her dear childhood friend, had lost her own caregiver and been forced into servitude with the Chisholms, the wealthiest family on the island, to earn her keep. Then, the accident that had disfigured Iona and killed her father five years ago only added to the legends surrounding her abilities to heal and she'd allowed those folktales to flourish to keep her privacy intact.

Some people believed her a witch based on the success of her ointments and tinctures for healing, while others knew her skills came from her parents, both healers and both now dead. Either way, the solitude she had chosen gave her a bit of peace and safety since her father's passing, as she was left to her own bidding to survive.

If townsfolk needed herbals, they left a note with coin in her box at the edge of her property. The next day, she would leave their herbs for them at their door in the cover of night. Such an exchange had helped her survive alone, which was exactly how she preferred it. The many animals she rescued and cared for at her cottage she understood, but most people she did not.

Although she cared for both deeply. Healing was in her bones and she could not keep from caring for any person or animal in need. It was against her nature, but on the other side of love was often loss, so she'd chosen to keep her heart to herself as much as possible.

She knelt at the man's side, gently brushing back

his dark hair from his face, revealing a nasty, bloody gash to the side of his temple. She turned him on his back and pressed her ear to his chest. A strong heartbeat greeted her and she closed her eyes in relief.

He was alive!

She prayed she might be able to keep him that way. She sat back on her haunches and studied him. He looked a handful of years older than her own three and twenty, but not too much older. Even with his eyes closed, his features possessed a seriousness about them as if he was prone to frown and worry. He was tall and muscular and so…large. How would she get him inside her cottage to care for him? She looked about him for solutions.

Sea netting was still tangled about his legs, ironically the very nets she had set out this morn in hopes of snaring some fish. She'd have to repair them anyhow, so what was a few more mends to make? She could use the nets to her advantage to drag him to the cottage. She'd hauled many a boat ashore and back… with great effort, but she'd done it. This man would be no different.

She fashioned the net as best she could to act as a cradle and began the task of dragging him along the shore behind her. Of course, the man was all muscle and weighed about fifteen stone if she were to hazard a guess. More than once, she fell on to her knees in the sand and rocks, scraping her legs, having to rest for a few moments before she could continue.

'By all that was holy,' she muttered, ignoring the pain from her bloodied shins. 'I will save you whether you wish to be saved or not.' She groaned from the effort and continued. Finally, they reached her door. The chill of before was long gone and she panted from the exertion. She pushed the door open. Half collapsing on the floor, she rested on her back, relieved she had him out of the elements.

The familiar padding of pawed feet resonated on the wooden floor and slobbery kisses lathered her cheeks. She laughed and reached up to pet her beloved hound. 'Jack,' she murmured. 'I am just as pleased to see you.' And she was. 'If only you were a small ox. Then you could have helped me haul in this man.'

But it was no matter. She had all but succeeded in her task. After catching her breath, she rose, dragged him fully inside and closed the cottage door. Then, she lit two candles, stripped off her soaked shift, dried off, put on a woollen dress and tied back her hair in a knot at the nape of her neck. She stood barefoot and studied the sight before her. 'What do I do with you now, kind sir?' She popped her hands to her hips. 'You do know how to fill a room, do you not?'

And he did. He consumed the entire entryway of her small cottage. She could not leave him in such a state, cold and wet on the floor. He would catch fever in no time and then he'd have an even lower chance of survival. Based on the gouge to his head, he'd need any advantage she could muster to stay alive.

Iona eyed her dwindling stack of wood and fuel for the fire by the hearth and glanced back at the man sprawled along her cold floor. While she'd already used her allotment of wood and kindling for the day, the man needed warmth and without a fire his clothes would never dry.

She nibbled her lip and after a moment's deliberation added a large log of wood and kindling to the hearth and lit it. Soon, the glowing flames crackled and yawned as the wood caught fire and lit up the room. She would do without later. For now, she needed to help this man live.

'Poor sot,' she murmured, glancing down at his fine face as the shadows and light from the fire danced along his features. A few additional cuts and scratches lanced his cheeks and neck, most likely from the sea and shoreline. She lifted his hands one at a time. They were impressive and strong, but nicked with small scars along the knuckles and a larger one that travelled up from the back of his hand disappearing under his jacket.

She rested his hand back on the floor. 'What brought you to our shores, eh? Not many strangers come to Lismore.'

She shrugged and began the arduous task of stripping the man down to his flesh. A task that should have daunted her, but it didn't. A man was just a man, was he not? And she had seen the bare male form before when Mother and Father had done their healings on men wounded in battle, often with one another, or with the sea. It had not impressed.

She tugged off his dark coat first, gently pulling his arm through one sleeve and then the other, careful to not injure him further in case there were additional wounds she could not yet see. It had been a fashionable jacket before spending such time in the water. She couldn't help but note the tailored cuffs and shining silver buttons. The man had means. She hung it by the fire to dry.

Then she carefully tugged his tunic from his trews, first the front and then the back, the fine soaked fabric transparent against his skin revealing a sculpted, handsome form she had never seen in a man. Carefully, she tugged it from over his shoulders and then his head, mindful of his wound there. Her fingertips trailed along his taut chest, broad muscular shoulders and arms, tracing along the dark tattoo of woven bands around his left bicep. His stomach even had muscles. A shiver scampered along her limbs.

Saints be.

If a man could be beautiful, he was. He had a raw, primitive power about him akin to a wolf.

The man must be a soldier, despite his fine clothes. Why else would he be so scarred and so fit for battle? She leaned over him and brushed the hair from his face. His strong, resolute features—a broad forehead, formidable nose and sharp jawline as if cut from a blade—reeked of confidence as if he was a man not to be trifled with.

'Who are you?' she asked. 'And why would you be tossed up on our shores?'

She hung his tunic and spied his jacket once more. The thieves could have missed something or been rushed in their pursuits when she came ashore. She prayed something, anything, might remain to reveal his identity. She searched the coat pockets, but found nothing.

As she hung it again by the hearth, her hand skimmed against something small and hard in the lining. Bringing it close to the fire, she discovered a brooch miniature of a young girl with auburn hair pinned into the side, close to where one's heart would be. A flutter of recognition captured Iona's attention.

Could it be? She gasped, bringing the miniature closer to the light of the fire.

Catriona.

Surely not. It looked like the childhood friend she had before her mother had died. A friend Iona had lost touch with shortly after she moved away from town and along the shore with her father. She shook her head. Her mind was playing tricks upon her. It could not be Catriona. The girl had no family other than the old woman who had raised her. Fatigue was getting the best of her. Iona set the small item aside on the table. Best to focus on healing him. Then she could ask him about the pin herself.

She knelt beside him and felt along his head for any other wounds and found only the sizeable knot she'd noted from the shore. He was lucky to have survived whatever had happened to him. It was a miracle he hadn't drowned. Most likely his fitness and strength had saved him. She caressed his cheek. 'Someone must be worrying over you,' she mused. 'I will do my best to see you returned to health and to them. I promise.'

She tugged off his boots one at a time and then

rolled down the soaked tights that gripped his flesh from below his knees to his large feet. The poor man's skin was pruned from being in the water so long. She dried his legs and feet as well as his upper torso and hair as best she could. Then she sucked in a breath and steeled herself before beginning to remove his trews. She peeled the heavy soaked material from his body.

Glory be.

He was a treasure among men. She blinked and commanded herself to focus on the task at hand rather than his impressive torso as she finished drying him off. She flushed and turned to a small trunk at the foot of the meagre straw mattress that served as her and Jack's bed. She'd long since given up banishing her hound to sleep elsewhere. The dog stared down at her from the bed as she rooted through what remained of her father's clothes. She held up the largest nightshirt to the stranger's substantial form and smiled.

'Ah. This shall do.' She shook it out and rested it on the trunk. It would cover most of him. Well, enough of him anyway.

She set a small pot of water over the fire, now that its flames were strong and steady. Next, she'd set about to clean the man's wounds and make the needed ointments and tinctures to aid in his healing. It would take hours and she had other tincture and herbal orders to fill, but haste was essential if the man had any hope of surviving.

After getting him settled, she'd worry about her orders and stay up all night if needed to fill them.

She couldn't go without coin to care for herself and her animals, especially when she was behind on her payments on the note that Chisholm held on her cottage…again. But she'd set aside such worries for now. She needed to focus on this stranger.

She studied him. He didn't look to be a fisherman or merchant. 'Are you a soldier?' she murmured. 'Perhaps rallying men to join the Jacobite Army?' she asked, adding another bandage. 'Although I do believe you were wearing a signet ring before that drunkard stole it from you…but you seem too scarred to be a laird?' she mused, cupping his cheek in her hand. 'You are indeed a mystery.'

The man moved, a subtle twitch of his face against her palm. She froze. Was he waking? 'Sir?' she pleaded. 'Can you hear me?'

He stirred, his eyes fluttering open, his soft brown gaze settling on her own. He reached out a shaky hand, held her cheek and quirked up a corner of his lip. 'You are beautiful,' he murmured, holding her gaze before his eyes closed and his arm fell back to his side.

Beautiful?

Shaken, she sat back on the floor. She pressed a hand to the scarred cheek he had touched, still tingling from his caress, and tears filled her eyes.

No man had said such a thing to her since her accident, let alone dared caress her disfigured cheek. The familiar ache of loneliness tightened her chest. Her mind spooled back to the pretend family and contented life she had imagined earlier this eve as she'd

floated out at sea and of the happy life she had once
had as a child so many years ago.

Do not be foolish.

She would be no one's wife, nor a mother. To love
was too great a risk—besides, who would have her
now that she was disfigured. Best to set aside such
longings and wishes that would never come true.
There was safety in being alone and she would keep it
that way. She blinked away her tears and set about fin-
ishing the task at hand. He was delirious. His words
meant nothing.

She looped her arms underneath his own and struggled to get the nightshirt on him. After two unsuc-
cessful attempts, she gave up and dragged his naked
and rather magnificent form to the bed, flopping him
headfirst on to the mattress raised but a few hands'
width off the floor. Soon, she had him turned over on
his back and tucked snugly under a woollen blanket
and quilt. His legs from the calf down protruded off
the end of her small bed. Popping her hands to her
hips, she sighed.

It was the best she could do. He was a very tall man.

She gathered up the rest of the man's wet clothes
and hung them before the fire to dry. She turned the
soaked tunic inside out, her fingers running along
some embroidery. Bringing it to the light, she saw a
word in dark thread: Royce. She glanced at the man
now sleeping in her bed.

'You could be a Royce, could you not? It is a fine
name. Given name or surname, I wonder?' She placed
it near the fire to dry, careful to keep it far from the

cinders, so the fine fibres did not catch aflame. Exhausted, she settled in on a makeshift bed on the floor near the fire. The orders would have to wait until tomorrow. She would wake early to make them and deliver them before first light. She always worked best in the morn anyway. Jack glanced at her on the floor and then jumped up on to the bed, curling up in a ball next to the man's side.

'Traitor,' she murmured as she snuggled down into her quilts. Although she couldn't blame the dog. She wouldn't mind sleeping snuggled up to the man either.

'Good night, Royce,' she said before she thought better of it.

She closed her eyes and fell asleep to the loop of his words even though she knew they would never be the truth.

You are beautiful...
You are beautiful...
You are beautiful...

Chapter Two

'*We have no further need of ye, Royce. 'Tis as simple as that,*' *the older man scoffed, his pock-marked face caught in the light of the full moon.*

'*This was not what you promised. I am here to see Webster. I will not leave until I do,*' *Royce growled, struggling against the man pinning his arms behind his back.*

'*Seems ye will be leaving after all,*' *the man answered with a laugh that his men echoed. 'Lads, help the good laird off the vessel. Fer good.*'

Royce strained to free himself, but it was too late. The four men overpowered him, each of them taking him by one limb. As he struggled, one of the men clubbed him in the head with the hilt of a sword. The world spun and blood blinded his vision in one eye.

The next thing he knew he'd landed in the water. He clawed and sputtered for the surface, trying to decipher the difference between the dark loch and the night sky. He shouted for help, gulping down a mouthful of water. The undercurrent picked him up and dashed him against the rocks and then everything faded to nothingness and silence…

Royce bolted up, panting for breath. He was on a bed…but it felt strange, as if it wasn't his own. He clutched at the scratchy, wool blanket around him and opened his eyes, attempting to decipher between what was a dream versus reality. His head throbbed in a sickening, sharp rhythm. It was dark, so dark, and the loud crashing of waves against rock echoed in his ears, but he was relieved to know he wasn't truly drowning. He was alive. He sucked in one breath after another, trying to slow his heart which thundered like horse hooves across a field in his chest.

Finally, his pulse slowed enough for him to take in his surroundings. It smelled of herbs, a light floral scent and…sickness. Gooseflesh rose along his skin, sending alarm through him. Something wasn't right. Where was he?

His thoughts were scrambled into fine bits of disjointed images and words, but his mind couldn't order them into any sense. He could remember being on a boat, arguing with the men there, then being in the water fighting for his life, but little more. And why couldn't he see anything? Surely, his eyes should have adjusted to the dark by now to see some grey edges here and there. A heavy weight pressed against his thigh, creating a dull ache. He moved his leg to ease the pain and an animal growled.

'Deuces,' he cursed, scrambling from the mattress, pulling down a small table and sending whatever was atop it crashing to the floor. Why was he trapped in a strange dark place with a wild animal? He went for his dagger. His palm hit his bare thigh instead of his waist belt and then his exposed chest instead of his tunic. He froze.

Where are my clothes? Why am I naked?

What the bloody hell was going on?

A dog barked and Royce backed away from the noise, lowering into a battle stance, putting out his hands to defend his body. The soles of his feet gripped the bare wooden floors for traction.

'Easy, boy. Easy,' he commanded, hoping the authority in his voice would calm the wild beast.

The dog barked again and nudged his wet nose to Royce's hand. He stilled. Was the damned beast merely wanting to play? Royce opened his palm and the dog slathered his hand with its tongue and released a playful yip. Royce exhaled, his shoulders relaxing as his arms fell to his sides. *Saints be.* He petted the dog's wiry hair and took a halting breath as his heart tried to regain a normal rhythm.

A latch clanked behind him followed by the slow, creaky opening of a door and Royce whirled around to defend himself, blinking rapidly to clear his vision, but still seeing nothing.

'Who are you?' he ordered, his voice stern and commanding as he felt about for a weapon, any weapon. His hand closed around what felt like a vase and he held it high in the air. 'And how dare you keep me prisoner here. Release me!'

'Sailor's fortune,' a woman cursed, followed by a clattering of items to the floor. 'I think my soul left

my body; you gave me such a fright. You are no prisoner,' a woman stated plainly. 'By all that's holy, cover
yourself. And put down the vase. It was one of my
mother's favourites.'

Bollocks.

Light footfalls sounded away from him, but Royce
stood poised to strike. He stared out into the darkness,
confused. Where was he and what was happening?
And why was some woman speaking to him as if she
knew him? Shouldn't she be as surprised as he was
to be here, naked and in her bed?

The door squeaked as it closed, followed by the
dropping of a latch.

'Then why am I here?' he demanded, still gripping
the vase, unwilling to set it aside for clothes. Staying
alive trumped any sense of propriety. She might not
be alone.

'I cannot say. You were face down in the sand when
I discovered you.' A pot clanged on what sounded to be
a stove. 'Would you care to put on some trews? They
are dry now.'

'Are you alone?' he asked, shifting from one foot to
another, staring out into the black abyss, still scared
and untrusting for he could not discern a thing in such
pitch-black darkness.

'Aye.' She chuckled. 'Except for my hound, Jack,
whom you have met.'

He relaxed his hold on the vase, felt for the mattress, and sat down, fighting off the light-headedness
that made him feel weak in the knees. He covered his

torso with the blanket and held his hand to the back of his head where he felt a lump.

His skull throbbed as if it might burst.

'Could I trouble you to light a candle if you do not plan to kill me? I cannot see a blasted thing and I would very much like to put on those trews you mentioned.'

Silence followed and then the tentative sound of footfalls on the floor. 'It is not dark in here, sir. 'Tis midday. I can see clearly with no candles lit. Can you not see me standing before you?' she asked, her words soft and cautious.

He stared before him and reached out, his hand falling through open space. 'Nay. I cannot see you,' he answered.

'Yet your eyes are opened,' she continued, concern edged her words. 'Perhaps the blow to your head caused a temporary lack of sight. Most likely it shall heal.'

'Blindness? I cannot be blind,' he complained. His heart pounded in his chest. He flinched at the feel of her feathery touch along his temple and instinctively gripped her wrist and held it away from his face to protect himself.

She stiffened in his hold, but didn't cry out.

'My name is Iona MacKenzie,' she said calmly. 'I will not hurt you. Nor will Jack—the dog has been huddled next to your side for days. I promise. You just need to allow your body time to heal. You need to trust what time can give you.'

Trust what time can give you.

Her words soothed him. He had no idea why. It was an odd turn of phrase. Perhaps a trick?

He scowled. For some reason, he believed her although he was entirely at her mercy and he had no wish to be at anyone's mercy. He ran his thumb along the inside of her wrist and her soft smooth skin felt good, far too good in his hold. He released her, letting his hand fall back on to the dog next to his side. He gave him a pet and then another, the feel of its coat a comforting certainty in all his confusion.

'Do you remember how you came to be here?' she asked.

He scoffed and ran his hand through his dirty hair, wincing at how much his head still throbbed. 'Nay. I cannot even remember who I am with this bloody headache.'

'I will make you a tonic.'

'Why should I dare drink it?' he asked, anger over his situation getting the best of him. 'You could poison me.'

'Poison you?' He heard footfalls across the room and a huff of frustration followed. 'Fine words from you after I dragged your arse in here and cared for you for days.'

'Days?'

'Aye. Three days you have slept. And, if I'd wanted to harm you, I would have just let you suffocate in the sand on the shoreline where I found you.' A pot clanged, followed by what he believed to be a quite unladylike curse. 'And to think, I even gave you my bed as I slept on the floor all this time,' she muttered.

'I have a mind to toss you from here and get on with my day. I have many other chores at present.'

Saints be. He flopped back against the mattress and pillow, pulling the blankets up and around his waist. The hound rested its head across Royce's stomach and sighed, knowing full well Royce's misstep. He couldn't help but chuckle at the rather obtuse situation he was in and how he'd dared to accuse *her* of poisoning him when she most likely saved his life... if she were telling the truth and his instincts told him she was. If she wasn't, she was a fine liar and unique accomplice to his capture.

He was wounded, couldn't see and could only remember his first name: Royce. Even that he was a bit uncertain of as it had only come to him in the harsh flash of memory that had awakened him but minutes ago. What right did he have to question anything she had done for him? He was being an arse. He laughed aloud at the absurd situation he was in.

'Are you laughing at me?' she asked, ire lacing her words.

'Nay. At myself. You saved my life, yet I complain like a child. I will repay you for your trouble.'

'You will?' she asked.

'Aye. I am sure I have the means to do so...once I remember exactly what those are and where I live.' His promise sounded ridiculous even to his own ears.

The clanging came to a halt. 'I thought you said you couldn't remember who you were?'

'I don't exactly, but I woke with a memory of being pushed off a boat into the sea. One of the men called me Royce and then "laird" before they threw me into the water.' He shuddered at the memory and his body quaked at the thought of being in the loch once more.

She approached and tugged the blankets up to his neck. 'A laird? Coming alone to this island?'

He frowned at the doubt in her voice. 'Aye, despite how odd it sounds.'

'Stay covered, so you won't get a chill,' she said as she tucked in the blankets. 'I would hate to have you die now after all the work we have put into your survival, whether you are a laird or not. Right, Jack?' Her fingertips skimmed along his shoulder, reminding him that he wore no tunic or any clothes at all. He froze. He'd briefly forgotten, but now he was keenly aware that he wore no clothes at all in the presence of this woman.

'Where are my clothes?' he asked.

'They are folded and in the trunk at the foot of the bed. They have been washed and mended as much as they could be. There were some large rips and tears. I will fetch them for you.'

'And you…removed them from me?'

'Aye,' she answered, matter of factly. 'You were soaked to the bone and would have died from chill if I'd left you in them. I live alone here. It was either I remove them, or you died.'

He said nothing. That was a first. Or was it? He rubbed his forehead, frustrated by his lack of memory. Why couldn't he remember? He squeezed his eyes shut to attempt to concentrate, which only made his headache worsen.

'You have quite a pleasing form, if I may say so, *my laird*,' she teased. 'You have nothing to be afeared of.'

He coughed and heat flushed his skin. Evidently, the woman was no shy flower, despite how young she sounded or how quickly her ire was plucked by his words.

She chuckled. 'I have not ever seen a man blush such before. Here I was thinking you to be a worldly creature.'

He nestled further under the blankets. What could one say to that? He risked directness. He'd already made an arse of himself. What more did he have to lose?

'And you have seen many a male form before?' he asked, his curiosity getting the better of him. He had no reason to want or need such information, but he found not knowing much about his past made him hungry to know everything about his present circumstances.

'Aye. I am a healer, or at least I used to be. Now I mostly prepare ointments and tinctures when people need them, or nurse wounded animals back to health.'

'Is that how you care and provide for yourself?'

'Aye. And I fish. I set out nets when I have need for them. It keeps me, Jack and the other animals fed, and the basics cared for, but little else.'

'Were you always alone?'

'Do you always ask so many questions?' she replied, a sharpness in her tone.

'Perhaps… I don't…remember,' he replied.

She didn't answer, but continued clanging about in what he assumed was the cottage's small kitchen.

His heart rate increased at the reminder of his situation. How would he ever get back to where he came from if he couldn't remember where that was? And how would he manage without his sight? And this woman…he didn't understand her. She lived alone and survived on making tinctures and what the sea gifted her. What kind of a life was that for a woman so young? Why wasn't she married? Had her husband died? Did she have no family? He opened his mouth to ask and clamped it shut. Clearly the woman invited no further questions.

But why? What was she hiding?

He spun what information he did have around in his mind, attempting to decide upon his next move. He could flee from the cottage in hopes of finding someone else to aid him in his recovery. Yet, how far would he get without clothes and sight?

He slowly sat up. He knew what he needed to do, even though the thought of it made his pulse skitter and his throat dry. Even if he didn't fully trust this woman yet.

'My apologies. I am grateful for your aid and hope you will help me get back home,' he said. His words came out raspy and awkward as if he'd never apologised before.

He swallowed hard. Perhaps he never had.

Chapter Three

Iona cringed and closed her eyes. *Blast.* The poor man was apologising.

Her father would be shaking his head at her. She'd always been a bit abrupt and quick to temper. Emotions ran high and low in her. One of the perils of living by her heart rather than her head. More than once she had spoken her mind and instantly regretted the words that fell from her lips. Today would be no exception, it seemed.

She hadn't meant for her words to be so sharp or insensitive. It had been a long time since she had someone who had asked her so much about herself. To be fair, this was the longest conversation she'd had with anyone in some time.

Deep down she knew he meant no harm and that he wasn't judging her like other villagers had in the past. By all that was holy, he couldn't even see her. He had woken up in a strange place not being able to see or fully remember who he was. If their roles were reversed, she would have been upset, confused and disagreeable as well. She took a deep breath and released it. She needed to make her own amends.

'Nay. I am sorry,' she offered. 'I am not so good with people sometimes. A hazard of living alone for so long. Of course you have questions. You woke in a strange place with no memory or sight. And I will answer the ones I can.'

'Is there anything you do know about me?'

She released a slow, steady breath and grabbed his clothes from the trunk. 'Based on your clothes, which I have here, I believe your name to be Royce, just like you said the men called you from your memory at sea,' she stated. 'It is sewn into the collar of your tunic. A given name, perhaps? Or surname?'

She touched his shoulder so as not to startle him and handed him his clothes.

'Royce,' he murmured as he took the garments, staring out into the distance. 'That is as fine a name as any although it triggers no other memories. Thank you for the clothes.' He pulled on his tunic, his muscles rippling along his abdomen. She bit her lip and turned away as he stood to slide into his trews. Although it didn't truly matter if she turned away or not, as he would be none the wiser, it mattered to her.

'I can take you to the outhouse if you need. Perhaps warm you some food and drink?' she asked, listening to the sounds of him tucking his tunic into his trews.

'Aye, to both,' he answered. The bed squeaked under his weight as he sat down.

She turned. He leaned forward with his elbows on his knees. 'I cannot fathom I am blind.'

''Tis temporary, I am sure,' she offered, although she was not nearly as certain as she sounded. She'd never known a man to be struck blind before. She did not know if his sight would return at all. She'd also been unsure if he would survive his initial injuries, but here he was awake and sensical, even if he had no memory.

He grunted and rose. 'Could I bother you to take me out to the outhouse?'

She cleared her throat and turned her back to him. 'Place your hand on my shoulder and walk behind me.'

His hand skimmed her neck and then his palm cupped her shoulder. The weight and firm pressure of his touch were surprisingly comforting. They took a few steps and then Iona paused. 'Step up so you can clear the threshold of the door. Then we will be outside. It is fine weather today. The sun shall do you much good after so many days indoors.'

As they breached the door and stepped out into the warm summer sunshine, his palm fell from her shoulder. She turned to find him lifting his face to the sun with his eyes closed. He breathed deeply, basking in the warmth like an otter on a rock before the shore.

Like a man lost and then found.

She swallowed hard and wrung her hands. She cursed herself. What was she doing with this man? He could not stay here in her cottage. She didn't even know who he was and nor did he. He could be a murderer, a liar, a cheat, or worse still…a rakehell. She shifted on her feet and narrowed her gaze at him.

But…he could also be a good, decent man in need of her help. A man who had suffered bad luck and needed one person to show him kindness.

Kindness costs nothing.

Her skin heated at the memory of her father's words to her many years ago when he'd tossed a crab back out into the water.

'Father, why do you bother to throw them back into the water when there are so many cast out after the storm? They will only be washed back out again after the next one,' she'd asked.

'Because such a kindness costs me nothing, while to that wee creature, it could mean everything.'

She could still feel his hand ruffling her hair and pulling her into his side as waves crashed along the shore littered with starfish, crabs, clams, and seaweed after the storm.

She'd paused and bent down to pick up a clam, cupping its smooth, cool shell in her hand. She'd run through the sand, letting the water lap up around her ankles and cast it out as far as she could, revelling in the subtle splash it made as it hit the water.

'You see,' he called. 'Your kindness cost nothing, and you made a difference to that wee creature.'

The fullness she felt in her heart that day had been contagious. She wanted to feel that she had made such a difference again and again and again. As she stared out at the shore at the stranger sitting in the sand, she realised he was her next clam. She would help him find his way back to the water, wherever such waters might be.

She could not send him out into the world with but one memory and part of a name. Father would turn in his grave at her selfishness and she would feel guilty the rest of her days. Her sense of decency wouldn't allow it. A breeze ruffled his hair and he spread out his arms, opening his palms to the sun almost as if he were a man in prayer asking for deliverance.

Then he opened his eyes and smiled. It was a small quirk of an upturned lip, hardly a smile at all really, but as bewitching a smile as she'd ever seen, and he looked right at her as if he could see. A dark lock of hair flopped over his eye and the opened V of his tunic revealed his rather handsome throat and chest once more. Her stomach dropped and she gripped the skirts of her gown.

Saints be. Why did he have to be so handsome?

She frowned.

Rakehell it was.

She'd be on guard until she figured out exactly what to do with him. His hands suddenly dropped to his side. 'What day is it? Where am I?' he called to her.

'It is a Thursday. The nineteenth of August 1745. And you are in Lismore. A small isle off the west coast of Scotland in Loch Linnhe.'

He nodded. 'Describe it to me,' he ordered.

When she was silent, he added, 'Please. I wish to imagine it.'

'I am unsure of where to begin,' she added, scanning the area. 'I have lived here all my life. It is like describing one's hands.'

He waited.

She cleared her throat, stared out as if with the new eyes of a stranger and began. 'It is rather lush, full of greenery, plants and flowers. Many people call it a garden isle as it is so fertile for planting, despite the hazards of the weather since we live so close to the sea.'

'What is it I smell?'

She smiled. 'Most likely the mixture of manure and my many herbs along with the loch.'

He chuckled. 'Ah. That explains it.'

'I care for all creatures, man or animal.'

'Alone?'

She squared her shoulders and ended his enquiry. She needed to keep her distance. 'Shall I take you to the outhouse?'

'Aye,' he answered and reached out his arm.

'Take a few steps forward.'

Once he had, she guided his hand to her shoulder. While she knew she shouldn't allow such intimacies, the building was a distance from the cottage and she didn't wish to undo all the healing she had accomplished by having him fall face first into the animal pen or end up in the loch.

'Almost there,' she murmured.

She stopped and he did as well. 'Reach out your hand and you will find the door handle. Do you need assistance?' she asked and then cringed. She had not meant to offer. The words just popped out unbidden.

He coughed. 'I'll manage.' His hand fell away and finally found the door handle.

As he pulled the door open, she offered, 'A basin with soap and water is to your left. The pot to your right.'

He hesitated. 'Thank you,' he answered and left her. *Curses.*

She turned away and stared out at the shoreline, the waters of the loch lapping against the pebbled coast. How did one help a blind man without sounding like a clucking hen? Crossing her hands against her chest, she shrugged. She supposed it was better than providing him no guidance at all and allowing him to fall face first into the pot.

One trifle at a time, little fish. No need to get ahead of yer challenges.

She smiled at the memory of one of her father's many lessons on life. He was right though. Why worry beyond the moment, especially with this man? She took in a slow breath, held it, then released it, which helped her heart to slow, matching the lulling tide as it made its way in. A storm would be moving in tonight. The darkening clouds gathered off in the distance and the musk of budding rain filled the air.

Jack charged past her and grabbed a piece of driftwood. He rushed back and dropped it to her feet. Iona flung the driftwood far out and the hound raced after it with unbridled enthusiasm.

The outhouse door clapped closed and she turned. Royce stood staring out before him, his hands outstretched, his facial features pinched in concentration as he took one small step and then another. She thought to call out to him, but held back. Perhaps she needed to allow him a few steps to gain his confidence before she rushed in to assist him.

She bit her lip and watched him take one step

and then another successfully. She smiled. Then he tripped over a root and fell, catching himself by putting his arms out to break his fall.

He cursed and she rushed to help him up.

'I am sorry,' she said, placing a hand under his arm to assist him. 'I had hoped to let you try first.'

He shrugged off her help. 'Nay. I am a grown man. I can manage,' he groused.

She stepped back. 'While I know you *wish* you could manage, you cannot. Not yet. You do not know the area. Let me help you. Once you learn where the path is, you will be able to manage on your own.'

'And why would you do that?' he scoffed. He gained his footing and brushed off his hands, wiping his palms down his trews.

She squared her shoulders. 'Because you need my help.'

'That is not an answer to my question.'

She tugged the shawl around her shoulders. 'I am unable to merely stand by and watch you struggle.'

He stilled. 'What? That is nonsensical.'

'Perhaps to you.' She lifted her chin. 'I have always been this way. If I find a bird with a broken wing, I help mend it. If there is a dog unfed, I feed it. If there is a woman with an ailment, I create a tincture. It is what I do, it is who I am and…' she added with more confidence, 'I find I am quite good at it.'

'And I am a bird with a broken wing to be mended, am I?' he griped bitterly, taking one unsure step after another.

She walked next to him, ready to catch him if he

started to fall. 'Nay. You are worse. You are a stubborn, arrogant man too proud to accept such help,' she grumbled.

He wavered and she grasped his bicep. He stilled and faced her, his dark brown eyes staring out past her as if he were searching for something or someone. 'Perhaps I am just a man who wished you would have left me to die upon that beach.'

Her chest tightened and she let go of his arm, stunned by his words. 'Is that truly what you wish?' she whispered, disbelief in her tone. 'You do not even know who you are and what life you may have to return to. Perhaps you have children or a wife. Siblings, even. If you are a laird as we believe you may well be, then you have a clan depending upon you.'

He also had a portrait of her beloved childhood friend Catriona. After days of staring upon the brooch, she was sure of it now. How did he know her? Was she alive? Happy?

She opened her mouth to ask all those questions, but stopped cold. Would such talk do anything other than upset him right now? Especially when he couldn't even see the miniature on his own.

'Aye,' he said bitterly. 'I have no memory, nor sight. At present, I am as useful as the seaweed and driftwood that surely clutters these shores. And certainly, if I had a wife and children, I would remember them.' He stumbled on towards the loch and half fell on to the sand and pebbles before sitting down on the craggy shoreline. Jack greeted him, dropped a stick in front of him, then leaned into his side.

Iona watched, clutching her shawl tightly around her chest willing Royce to accept the sweetness her hound offered. Willing him to show her he wished to live after all, no matter the difficulty of his situation.

For a man who wished to die couldn't be saved. That was a lesson she had learned long ago from her parents when they were healers.

Pet him, she prayed. *Pet him.*

She waited.

Jack rested his furry head on Royce's shoulder.

Iona held her breath. Still the man didn't move. Gentle waves rushed in on the shore, one after another in a soft rolling cadence. The smell of the sea and the gentle breeze ruffled his dark hair and the thin fabric of his tunic. Her breathing slowed. Still the man didn't move.

Please, pet him.

And after a few more moments, Royce lifted his hand from the sand and tentatively stroked the dog's wiry coat once and then again before wrapping his arm around him in what was close to a hug.

Iona sighed and bit her lip, tears burning her eyes.

Jack had saved her once, too, right after her father's death. Perhaps the sweet beast could work his magic once more.

Chapter Four

Royce gripped the wiry fur of the dog beside him. Rage coursed through his blood. While he couldn't remember who he was or why he was here on this little isle of Lismore, he couldn't imagine that any of this was to plan. He was blind with a solitary scrap of memory to claim as his own. All he knew for certain was he didn't belong here and he was alone.

He chided himself. Well, he wasn't entirely alone, was he? He had this beast of a dog and a woman hell-bent on saving him even though he wasn't quite certain he wished to be saved at all. He was a burden, plain and simple. Why couldn't the woman see that?

He ran his hand down Jack's fur and the dog sighed against him.

'Aye,' Royce whispered. 'She is set on saving me, isn't she? Is that what happened to you, too?'

The dog licked his face and Royce smiled. 'I know I should be grateful to be alive. I'm just not ready to be.' For now, all he wanted was to be angry about his situation. *Very* angry.

He breathed in the smell of the sea, the sweet grass, and the dampness of the air. A storm was coming in. That he knew. But how did he even know it? Why could he remember and know such trivial bits such as when the weather might be turning, but not his full name or what he even looked like? Did he have dark or light hair? Was he tall or short? Did he even like dogs or did he prefer horses? He scrubbed a hand down his face. Did it even matter? His stomach growled. Well, one thing he knew for certain. He was starving. Heaven knew the last time he had eaten.

Jack stiffened against him, his thin muscular body suddenly tense. Royce stilled as well and listened, but he heard nothing. Jack nudged his snout under Royce's shoulder once and then twice before standing and barking, alerting to some unknown danger.

Another dog barked in the distance, answering Jack's alarm, and then Royce heard it: the voices of men. They were too far off for him to be able to distinguish their words, but there were many.

Something was amiss.

'Come inside!' Iona called, her voice drawing nearer until she was at his side. She placed a hand upon his shoulder. 'I know not what they want. I get few visitors for I live far away from town. Make haste!' she hissed close to his ear.

'Why do I need to run from them? They may know who I am,' he said, confused by her alarm. 'They could help me.'

'Trust me on this.'

Something in her voice made him heed her warning.

He scrambled up and she grasped his hand. The feel of her strong yet delicate palm against his own tugging him urgently along set his pulse racing. Not much seemed to ruffle the woman, so her urgency concerned him. He hustled along as best he could, knocking into her side at one point, as she led him stumbling across the sand and up a hill back into the warmth of the cottage. He tripped over the small lip on the door threshold and crashed into her, sending them against the wall of the cottage with a thud.

Her soft form pressed full against his own, reminding him not all of him was dead and not everything he knew about life had been erased. Attraction and desire flashed through him at the feel of her soft hair against his cheek and the smell of the light floral scent of her skin. His hands lingered longer than they should have along her torso and he felt her breath hitch.

Too soon, she extricated herself from him. He heard the door close and the latch drop.

'You must hide.' She clutched his hand and dragged him along, his knee crashing into the bed corner, and he cursed. 'Careful,' she murmured a bit too late.

He rubbed his knee and stumbled beside her.

'Crouch down behind the bed and I will cover you with a quilt,' she ordered.

'Who are they?' he asked as he felt for the bed and slid to the cool floor. 'Why do I need to hide? I have done nothing wrong…that I know of.'

'Townsfolk often mean no harm,' she whispered. 'But few ever come to see me and there seem to be a pack of them, so something is amiss. And I'd rather hide you than find out too late that it is you they seek.'

'Why would it matter if they found me?'

'It might not, but they have the hounds with them. That only happens when they are searching for someone lost or someone dangerous. They may believe you are neither...or both for you are a stranger to us.'

He gripped her wrist. She still wasn't answering him. 'Why would it matter?'

'We are a small isle and the men here are fiercely protective. Even of a woman such as me.'

His brow knit in confusion. A woman such as her? What did that even mean? 'Why would they not be?' he asked.

'Shh. Trust me. Hide.'

Did he have any other choice? He was at the woman's mercy. She threw the quilt over him and he huddled down into it. He took in deep breaths until his heart slowed and then he set to listening as if his life depended on it. For all he knew, it did.

Long minutes passed without anything. His mind raced. He could reveal himself. The men might know who he was and why he was here. He frowned. Or they could be responsible for tossing him into the sea and almost drowning him. There was no way to know for certain. The woman had kept him alive so far. He would trust her...for now. A loud knock sounded and he held his breath.

'Aye,' she answered, her voice smooth and even. The latch scraped along the wood and the door squeaked open.

'Afternoon, Miss MacKenzie,' a man said in a deep heavy burr.

'Mr Chisholm,' she replied. 'A beautiful day.'

'Better than most,' he answered.

'In need of a poultice or tincture?' she asked.

'Not today. Wanted to check on your well-being. Heard a man was washed up along the shore a few days ago, but there's no sign of him now.'

'Really?' she asked.

'Aye. The lads said you interrupted them from thieving from him.'

'Aye. I did.'

'They were far too deep in their cups and feel poorly about what they did, which is why we only learned of the event today and organised a search,' he continued. 'You know what became of the man? There have been no sightings of him since that eve, which has us wondering if he was dead after all, or if we need to be on the lookout for him. Could be he is dangerous.'

Royce stiffened. *Saints be.* Men had been pillaging from him on the shoreline and *she'd* intervened? He fisted his hands. He didn't know if he was more angered at the men stealing from him or her risking her life in trying to keep them from doing so on her own. She could have been killed. He commanded himself not to burst up and demand names. He was blind. He didn't even know exactly who he was. He could do nothing to defend her honour or his own.

His heart thundered in his chest, and he had to concentrate to hear their words over the sound of it.

'Odd,' she answered. 'His body should still be there. I merely interrupted their thievery to grant the poor man some peace and dignity, much as my father deserved but was denied when he was also found along that shoreline, stripped of most of his possessions. Surely you could understand that.' Her words held a sharpness Royce had not heard before.

'Aye.'

'Could he have been pulled back out to sea?' she offered after another beat of silence. 'It was quite a high tide that eve and a storm came in shortly after. This summer has been rife with them rolling in one after another.'

Royce pressed his lips together and lifted his brow. Why on earth was she lying for him and putting herself at risk? There was no need to, was there? This woman was a puzzle to him. One he was eager and yet almost frightened to discern. Something about her fearlessness and independence intrigued him far more than it should. He did not even know her. If she perished from trying to protect him, he would not be able to forgive himself.

'Could be,' another man added. 'Storm did blow in that night.'

'Well, keep an eye out,' Chisholm added. 'Especially if you start missing livestock or food. The man could be alive and may be dangerous if he is trying to survive on his own on the island.'

'Aye,' the other man said. 'Best latch yer door and be watchful. Listen to good ol' Jack here.'

She chuckled. 'I always do. He has saved me on

more than one occasion. Thank you for your concern and for letting me know to be alert and watchful in the coming days.'

'Of course. Just because yer out of town it doesna mean we don't wish to keep ye safe, Miss. We'll be travelling up to the end of the shoreline and circling back later this eve. If you remember anything else or see anything suspicious between now and then, let us know when we swing back through.'

'Aye. I will. Thank you again for stopping by. And be careful.'

'And, Miss MacKenzie, I'll be expecting the payment on your note by week's end,' Chisholm added, his pitch lower. 'You are a month past due.'

Royce shifted. Past due? She had not enough for herself and spared what she had upon him. Why was this woman risking such for him?

'Aye, Mr Chisholm. And I am grateful for the extra time. I will bring payment on to you in full by the end of the week.'

'Pleased to hear it. Good day,' he answered.

The door closed and the latch dropped. Then Iona muttered a curse. 'Foul man.'

Questions and emotion swirled in Royce, but he also knew he needed to wait until the men were further away before he burst out with his enquiry in case they were still watching. His situation was far more precarious than he thought. People knew he was here, but didn't trust his intentions because he was a stranger. Could he blame them? *He* didn't even know his intentions for being here.

What could have brought him here? And who the bloody hell was he? While he had part of his name, Royce, it was a far cry from knowing who he was, where he lived and why he was here on this tiny island.

''Tis safe now,' she said. 'They are out of sight.'

Royce threw off the quilt. 'Why did you risk your life intervening against a pack of drunken men, especially when you believed me dead?' he asked, grasping for the bed to help himself stand. 'You could have been killed,' he groused, his words sounding far harsher than he intended.

'I could not leave you there being picked over by those men as if you were rubbish. It was what happened to my father. I could not leave you to such a fate.'

'Your father?'

'Aye. There was a horrible boating accident a few years ago. A storm came upon us quickly before we could get back to shore. The boat overturned and we were separated. He was lost to the sea, only to be washed up a few days later. Then, those scoundrels pillaged him as if he were...' She didn't finish. 'It doesn't matter. It was long ago.' A log shifted in the hearth.

It was obvious it still pained her despite how much time had passed, but he let the matter drop.

'And why are you lying for me?' he asked quietly. 'Why not tell them I am here? There is no need for you to put yourself at greater risk on my behalf.'

'Because it is my decision to do so and I know these men. You are a stranger. You would serve as an easy answer to any problem along these shores.'

Silence settled between them. Her distrust of the people in her community was evident in her tone. It begged another question as to why, but he wasn't sure she would welcome such an enquiry.

'If you are late on your note on this dwelling, you should not be exerting your efforts on saving me. I can find my own way.'

'Why are you lecturing me on my choices? You are not my father, or my husband. You are also no prisoner. Leave if you wish. If you want to chase after them and reveal yourself only to be killed by them later for a crime you didn't commit, then go ahead. I will not stop you.'

Bollocks.

'I was merely trying…' He paused.

'Well, please stop,' she quipped.

What *was* he trying to do? She was right. He wasn't her husband or father. But the thought of her putting herself at risk for him stirred something deep in his gut he didn't wish to name. Her care for him made him uncomfortable, vulnerable even, as if she was giving him something he would never be able to repay. He didn't wish to owe her anything. He didn't wish to owe anyone.

He felt for the bed and sat down. Jack rested his head on his knee and Royce pet the dog's furry neck.

Not knowing what to say, he sat in silence.

'I will put on some stew,' she murmured. 'You must be starved.'

Royce listened as she worked, trying to become accustomed to the fact that while he could not see, he could still hear and feel the air moving about as she walked by. Perhaps if he focused on that more than his own rage and frustration for a few minutes, his mind would clear.

He heard her chopping what he assumed were vegetables. He could feel the warmth of the fire in the hearth and smell the beginnings of a broth cooking.

'How do you know I am not a criminal or a murderer?' he asked, running his hand absently over Jack's fur.

Her steps faltered and then continued. 'Well, are you?' she asked.

'Not that I remember.'

'If you were a murderer or criminal, you would have showed your true self by now. You have had ample opportunity to lay siege upon me and this cottage, but you have done neither. Besides, Jack likes you and he is a fine judge of character.'

He nodded.

'If anything, I believe someone tried to kill *you*. Such blows to the head and body do not come about from a knock about in the sea. I am more concerned about who that may be and if they know you are still alive.'

He shifted on the mattress. Such a realisation unsettled him. Someone tried to kill him? Why?

'You believe I am in danger?' he asked.

'I do. I have had days to puzzle out theories as to how you may have come to wash up on our shores.'

'And those are?' he asked, interested in her thoughts.

'You truly wish to know?' she asked. Her words brimmed with hesitation.

'Aye. I do.'

'Well, first, there was a storm after you washed ashore, but not before, so it could not have been a boat accident. Second, one of your wounds to the head was severe. The bump was not one a person might incur from a rock or a fall from a cliff. I believe someone struck you at close range. Perhaps you knew them.'

Someone he knew? Attacking him? With the intent to kill?

It was too much to consider all at once. His pulse increased and his head throbbed in that same dull sickening rhythm as when he first woke. His stomach cramped. He pressed his fingertips to his temples to try to ease the pain and sickness with little success.

'Does your head still pain you?' she asked, her voice softening.

'Aye,' he murmured. 'Almost as much as my uselessness.'

She walked over and the mattress dipped as she sat next to him. 'Face me,' she whispered.

He did as she asked and turned to her, his knee touching her own, her soft floral scent becoming familiar and comforting. She rested her hands gently on his own and pulled them away from his forehead.

'Let me,' she whispered.

He hesitated and then settled his hands in his lap, willing himself to relinquish control and allow her to help him. The warm pads of her fingertips rested on his temples and then moved in small circles, the pressure just right. He sighed aloud at the relief it brought and closed his eyes.

'My father used to do this for my mother when she had horrid megrims. It always worked.' There was that smile in her voice again. How he wished he could see it.

He stilled. Where had that thought come from? What was he doing? He had no right to wish anything, especially when he had no idea of who he was or what life he already had. He set the thought aside. His worries were useless.

The pounding in his head was easing back with every circle against his temples. 'You are a gifted healer,' he murmured. 'Thank you.'

Her circles stopped and then began again. 'Thank you,' she answered in kind.

'Who taught you such skills?'

'My mother at first. She learned from my grandmother, who knew all there was to know about plants and herbs. My mother and I used to spend days looking for different plants to dry and store for her tinctures, and she made such searches into adventures.'

'Sounds like an amazing woman.'

'She was.'

'When did she die?' he asked, knowing full well that he had no right to ask. It was none of his business.

The circles stopped. 'When I was seven. From fever. My father and I tried, but we could not make any tincture that would help her.'

'I am sorry,' he whispered.

She rose from the bed, her loss immediate and sudden. 'It was a long time ago.'

It didn't seem like it to him. Sorrow tugged at her words.

He wondered what kind of woman lived alone by the sea taking in those who needed care without hesitation. Despite not knowing who he was, he knew he was not as sacrificing as her.

'I will check on the stew,' she added. 'It should be almost ready.'

He opened his mouth to ask about her father, but thought better of it. They hardly knew one another. He scoffed. He hardly knew himself.

'Was there anything that you found with me? Anything that hadn't been plundered?' he asked. Perhaps there was some small clue within what little remained of his so-called life before now.

'I know the men took a ring from you. I suppose it was a signet ring if your memory is correct and you are indeed a laird.' There was a pause in her voice and he waited.

'And?' he added, wondering about her hesitation.

'There was a small miniature sewn into your jacket. It is of a young girl. A daughter, perhaps? Or someone you loved and lost?'

'A daughter?' His chest tightened. 'I do not feel like a father,' he murmured.

She chuckled. 'Does one feel like a mother or father?' she asked.

He shrugged. 'I do not know, but I would like to think I would remember such an important part of myself even if I had been struck unconscious. May I see it?' He scrubbed a hand down his face. 'I know I cannot see it, per se, but can I hold it?'

'Of course,' she answered. 'It is your possession, not mine.' Footfalls followed her words and she returned to him. She clutched his hand and placed a small oval in his palm. His brow furrowed.

He closed his fingers over it and felt a small delicate clasp. 'Is it a brooch?'

'Aye,' she answered softly.

'Hmm. Why would I have had a brooch fashioned from a portrait miniature?'

'A fine question.'

'I want to imagine her. Will you describe her for me?' His thumb rubbed over the small portrait in his hand.

'She has long auburn hair and a rather petite face and features. And her eyes are quite bewitching. They are almost golden. A beautiful girl.' Her voice was wistful as if she was remembering the girl as well.

'Golden eyes. Sounds quite beautiful. Are any of her features like my own? What do I look like?'

'You are tall…' she paused '…and quite…muscular. Your features are dark, menacing even. But you are handsome.'

He found himself holding his breath for her to continue. What she thought of him mattered, but why?

'You have black hair and dark brown eyes." She paused and continued. "There is an odd kindness in your eyes actually.'

'Oh?' he asked, intrigued by her turn of phrase once more.

'Aye. As if you do not wish anyone to know you have a heart.'

The emotion in her voice seized him and he stilled. Did he?

'While her features are petite and lighter, yours are more stark and severe. You have the sharp, quick responses of a soldier. The scars as well.' Her fingertips grazed a ridged scar from his hand up to his forearm and her touch sent a quiver through him. 'This one is quite severe.'

He cleared his throat and moved on. 'Perhaps she is not my daughter at all,' he murmured, his fingers halting their movements over the brooch as another thought occurred to him. 'Could I have been charged to find her?'

'As a laird? Why would you do that? Surely you would send someone else in your stead.'

'Not if she was important. She could be family. Lost…like me.'

Chapter Five

Tell him.

Iona bit her lip and paused, holding the full ladle of stew over the wooden bowl, steam rising through the air. She *knew* she should tell him who she believed the portrait of the girl was and stop these ridiculous fabrications of it possibly being his daughter, but every time her lips parted to utter the words, no sounds came out.

It is too soon.

The unfortunate man just awoke after three whole days of sleep and was recovering from a serious head injury. And what if she was wrong?

Her gut twisted at her own denial. She *knew* the girl was Catriona. Those eyes were distinctive and unique. She could lie to herself all she wished, but that miniature was of her childhood friend. And didn't she owe it to the man to be honest?

It could help him remember.

The stew cascaded into the wooden bowl fashioned by her father's own hands.

The truth will never betray you, little fish.

Iona wasn't so certain. She emptied another spoon-ful of stew into the bowl. 'The stew is ready,' she of-fered, squaring her shoulders. She resolved to tell him the truth…after he ate.

'Smells heavenly. Thank you,' he answered.

'There is a small table with two chairs where we can sit. Take five steps forward and you will feel a chair before you,' she instructed.

He walked forward and rammed his knee into the chair, causing the table to shift.

He grimaced and clutched the top of the back of the chair while he rubbed his kneecap.

She cringed. 'Apologies. Make that four. I must remember how much taller you are than I am and adjust my guidance.'

'Nay. I will figure it out. Do not trouble your-self.' He placed the miniature gently on the table and sat in the chair. Iona's gaze rested on it briefly and she smiled back down at her old childhood friend's sweet face.

What if he did know her? What if after all these years, Iona could be reunited with her? Catriona had been one of her dearest friends as a child. The one person who had dared visit her after they moved to this remote part of the island and who would sit in silence with her along the shore as they carved their names in the sand. They had both lost a great deal at such a young age and they understood one another's grief in a way no one else could. What if they were back in each other's lives as adults? A glimmer of hope rather than fear ignited in her gut.

She set a small loaf of bread before him with what butter she had left. She would need to make more this week, but her time had been scarce while tending to him and making her tinctures.

She almost lifted a slice of bread to butter it for him and then thought better of it. He was not a child. If he was to learn to adjust to his lack of sight, she had to allow him opportunities to learn and gain confidence on his own. 'There is butter and bread to the right of your bowl of stew, if you wish.'

'Thank you. It smells delicious. I can truly say I do not remember the last time I ate.' A flicker of that almost-smile came and went in the blink of an eye.

Her gaze lingered upon him. 'It is remarkable how much you have recovered in a day. Miraculous even.'

He picked up the spoon, but then set it down. He lifted the bowl carefully, guiding it to his mouth and drank the stew from the bowl in hearty gulps. She paused, equally surprised and amused. She'd not even thought of it. Soon, he set it down and felt about for the bread, not even bothering with the butter, before wiping a piece around the bowl, sopping up the juices and broth that remained, before eating it.

He ate like a man starved, which perhaps he was.

She gaped at him because she could.

When he set down the bowl, he wiped the edges of his mouth with his hand, leaned back against the chair and sighed. 'Most delicious stew I've ever had.'

'Perhaps the only stew you can remember eating,

but thank you,' she answered, uncertain what to do next. She'd not even touched her food yet. 'Would you like more?'

'Aye, but not now. I will wait for you to finish first. Apologies for my haste.' He picked up the small miniature again, rubbing his thumb over it as if it were a worry stone. She took a bite of bread.

'I cannot stay here,' he stated as she chewed. 'It is not proper. You are an unmarried woman, are you not?'

She shrugged and stirred her stew as she swallowed her bite of bread. 'Aye, I am not wed, but it is no matter.'

His hand stilled over the brooch. 'But shouldn't it matter? What will your neighbours think? I am unsure why you risked hiding me at all. If they discover me, you will be ruined.'

'I do not worry about such trifles. I am not exactly a lady of the loch. It has no bearing to me. I have no reputation to lose.'

'Why not?'

'It simply does not matter to me what they think. I prefer to be alone anyhow.'

'You prefer it?'

'Aye. I have been alone five years since my father died. It is not so bad.'

'It doesn't sound so good either.'

Says the man with no memory.

She bit back the thought. 'It is good enough,' she countered.

'It sounds lonely.'

'My animals provide me company and I am busy

keeping up with the many chores I must attend to and tinctures I prepare. Here I answer only to myself and I have all I need. I find the solitude peaceful.' She stiffened at the sharp edge in her voice. Why was she defending herself? Why did she care what he thought? She did not know him and he would soon be on his way, living another life as soon as he remembered what that life was.

She glanced back at the miniature still clutched in his hand. Telling him of Catriona might help him regain his memory and help her discover answers as to what had become of her sweet friend, but still she hesitated.

Deep down she feared the truth: what if she had lost yet another person she loved? What if Catriona was dead? Iona swallowed hard. Just like her mother and father. She forced down another spoonful of stew.

Royce stared off in the distance. His brow furrowed once and then twice before he crossed his arms against his chest and spoke. 'So, you would allow me to stay on?' he asked. 'Until I determine who tried to kill me and who I am? Until my sight and memory return?'

She paused. 'Perhaps,' she answered, uncertain of what he would ask next.

'What if I helped you with your chores and tinctures? Perhaps there are even repairs I could attend to in the cottage. I know I cannot see, but I may still be able to help you, I think. I could then repay you later once I determine who I am exactly.'

'Why would you wish to do such? Wouldn't you

be compromising *your* fine reputation, since you believe you are a laird?' She did not bother to hide the sharpness in her words.

Unruffled, he nodded. 'A fair response, but I could not help but overhear the comment about your overdue note for your home. It seems you need help as much as I.'

Her cheeks heated. She didn't realise he'd heard that bit. She *was* overdue on her note to Chisholm and it plagued her to think about it. This cottage was all she had left of her father, her family, her connection to the past. If it were gone, would she also blow away and disappear into the wind like the downy tuft from a dandelion?

'I did not mean to embarrass you,' he murmured, his words soft and husky, as if he'd regretted them.

'Who says I am embarrassed?' she countered.

'I may not be able to see, but I can almost hear it in your silence. You are proud, like me.' He uncrossed his arms and leaned forward towards her.

She frowned, shifting in her chair. The truth in his words grated on her. How did this man know anything of how she felt? Or what she was like?

And, more importantly, why did he care? Why did she?

'I cannot take your charity without repayment,' he continued. 'And it seems I could help you. Surely there are some tasks that you cannot do because of your size and lack of strength.'

'You think you—' she said and he interrupted her

by reaching out his hand to her, but not quite reaching her arm. His palm rested on the table instead.

''Tis not a slight, Miss MacKenzie, but truth. You are strong, I am sure, but petite. Even you must confess to some limitations even if it pains you. Just as I must accept my present limitations as much as it pains me.'

There was that bloody smirk again. She wished to erase it from his face. Nay, that wasn't quite true. She sighed. Perhaps just the arrogance that accompanied it.

'Think of it as an arrangement that benefits us both,' he continued. 'Even though it may plague you to teach me to do such tasks and crumble my pride to bits to have to let you, I believe we can help one another.' An edge of humour entered his voice and she couldn't help but smile.

He had a point.

'I am quite sure you shall plague me in a variety of ways,' she quipped, a smile getting the best of her, 'but you are right, we could benefit from one another's help. I cannot lose my home and you cannot manage without me at present.'

'And it shall not be permanent,' he rushed out. 'A temporary endeavour until my sight and memory return or the mystery of who attacked me and how I came to be here is resolved.'

She had risked all by lying for him already. She set down her spoon. What were a few more days or weeks? She had nothing to lose. She stared upon him, his profile in the dwindling eve light resolved and serene. She'd need to light the candles soon. Perhaps he could help her earn enough to get ahead in her payments to Chisholm.

'You are quick to accept your new situation,' she stated. 'I find it intriguing.'

'Is there another option?' he replied.

'Nay. I suppose not.'

'Then, what is your answer? Do we have an agreement?' He extended his open hand to her.

Had he lost everything before?

Perhaps that was what made him so capable of adjusting to a new and unexpected future.

The realisation of such a possibility stilled her as she recalled the many scars on his body she'd noted while tending to him. There were some parts of the past that could not be erased.

A painful truth she knew and understood. The fact that he might also know moved her.

She stretched out her hand and slipped her small petite palm into his own and gripped it.

'Aye,' she answered. The word resonated in the tiny room with significance and her pulse increased from the sweet pressure of his warm hand around her own.

A flutter of awareness made her breath catch in her throat. He released her hand and she fisted it to hold the warmth and tingling before it faded away. A flash of remembering his hands upon her torso earlier heated her body.

'May I have another bowl?' he asked.

She blinked back her imaginings and returned to

the present. Standing, she cleared her throat. 'Aye,' she answered and picked up his bowl.

None of it mattered. He would be on his way soon enough and they would return to their own lives with their paths never intersecting again. Her attraction to him would be a fleeting fancy from being alone for so long. It would fade once she became used to him and then he would soon recover and be gone from these shores.

'We will have to be careful of when you are out, so you are not seen,' she said, ladling stew into his bowl, focusing on the present. 'Although I have few visitors, we will have to be watchful of them. It is a small town. Once you are spotted, they will come for you and without such pleasantries next time. Chances are they will also punish me for hiding you. Both of us will be in danger if you are noticed.'

She walked over and set the bowl down before him.

He reached out and rested his hand around her forearm. 'I understand the risk you are taking and I am indebted to you. I promise you that I will do nothing to put you in further jeopardy.'

She stiffened.

'Perhaps you shouldn't make promises that you may not be able to keep.'

'I don't.' His thumb caressed her arm absently, as if he did not even know he was doing it.

A small trail of fire ignited there, his touch to her skin like dry tinder set aflame in the hearth. Her breath hitched. 'Then you shall have to stay indoors during the day and emerge only at night when the shadows can hide you.'

His hand fell away into a fist at his side.

'That matters not to me,' he said bitterly. 'All of it is darkness.'

Chapter Six

The second crack of thunder sounded and Jack huddled up close to Royce as he sat at the small table. The dog shivered against Royce's thigh and leg, his furry head nestled across his lap. 'Not a fan of storms, eh?' he said, running his hand through the dog's fur.

Iona chuckled. 'He came to us on a night just like this years ago, didn't you, Jack? Found him scratching at the front door. I opened it and he burst in. As you can see, he never left.'

There was that smile in her voice again. Royce found himself smiling back.

He listened to her footfalls, trying to imagine the small cottage and what she was doing. Such imaginings proved a decent distraction until he realised why he was doing it: because he couldn't see.

A louder boom shook the small cottage. Jack pawed Royce's leg.

'Soon, he will be in your lap like a baby,' Iona added. 'Here, cover him with this blanket. Not seeing the lightning will help.' A soft blanket grazed his hand and he took it, covering Jack as best he could. Soon, the dog stopped shaking, but still pressed against him, seeking comfort.

Royce knew exactly how Jack felt.

Afraid.

Royce's world was darkness and he hated it. But he couldn't decide what he wished to gain back more: his sight or his ability to remember exactly who he was. It didn't really matter. He couldn't snap his fingers and have either back. Best to be present and focus on what he did have: shelter, food and the kindness of a woman and dog he barely knew.

The feel of Jack pressed against him anchored him to this time and place. That and the sounds and smells of this cottage, namely Miss MacKenzie. *Iona*. Such a simple name for such a complex woman. Listening to her movements in the cottage helped ease some of the loss and confusion, but her touch did something else to him entirely and he'd be wise to remember such.

Even though he couldn't remember who he was or his life before him, he'd be a gentleman now despite the attraction the feel of her soft, supple form stirred in him. And the smell of her was something soft and subtle, its floral and earthy hints a promise of the unknown and known all in the same breath.

He'd do well to keep his distance.

'I shall return,' she said, interrupting his thoughts. 'I must tend to the animals outside and ensure the gates and hutches are secured. This storm is coming in fast.'

He lifted his arm to object and offer to do it himself, but clamped his mouth closed, letting his arm fall to his side. Fool. Without sight, he would be nothing but a hindrance to her.

Just like you always were.

He stilled. A memory of an older man uttering such words to him flashed briefly in his mind before disappearing. He frowned. That couldn't have been his father, could it? Surely such words would not have been spoken to him in such cruelty. But who did say it? His mind clawed back, reaching for more, but nothing came. He pounded his fist on his thigh, startling Jack, who whined in protest.

'Sorry. Easy, boy,' Royce whispered. 'You are safe. I'll protect you.'

Being able to protect the wee creature made him feel some small sense of worth. It didn't matter that it was merely a dog.

The cottage door whipped open, clapping back against the wall of the cottage with a thud. 'You must hide,' Iona ordered. 'They return.' She slammed the door, yanking the blanket away from Jack briefly to help Royce up. Then she pushed him along, guiding him to behind the bed once more. He stumbled, half tripping over his own boots.

'Under the bed this time. And cover yourself with this.' He grabbed the blanket she thrust at him and shimmied under the bed, a tight and uncomfortable squeeze, but he managed it. He covered himself and felt the mattress above him sink as Jack jumped atop it.

Smart dog.

Minutes later, there was a loud knock at the door, which Iona waited a beat to answer.

'Gentlemen,' she said. 'Quite a storm to be out and about in.'

'Just wanted to make sure you were all buttoned this eve before the weather blew in, Miss MacKenzie. Need any help?' a man offered.

'Nay, Mr Chisholm. I just checked to make sure the barn and hutches were latched shut and all was secure. The animals are restless from the weather, but in all other accounts fine.' There was a tightness in her voice Royce did not like. The men would notice it as he did. Hopefully they would think it mere stress of the storm. He believed it to be otherwise, but from what? He stilled, straining to hear.

If only he could see what was happening.

'Any luck with your search?' she asked.

'No one has seen anything of note or the man at all. 'Tis as if he disappeared from this isle just as mysteriously as he appeared, but we won't give up. Not yet.'

'I hope not.'

'Best we get on before the storm rages in full. The wind and waves are whipping up somethin' fierce. Be careful. Good eve,' he offered.

'Safe travels,' she said and closed the door, quickly dropping the latch to secure it.

Royce shifted, preparing to get up.

'Stay hidden, right, Jack?' she said aloud. 'This storm is a nasty one. Best be still and ride it out.'

He froze. She was signalling him to stay put, but why? He listened as she moved about the cottage.

Bowls and pots were washed and stacked as she cleaned up and soon she sang a sweet tune, the likes of which he thought he recognised, but from where? He stayed hidden, his body aching from the tight confines.

The storm increased in intensity and rain battered the cottage, the sound loud and echoing within. The wind howled outside and the mattress above shifted. Jack appeared next to Royce, shaking. The dog pressed so closely to Royce that he wondered if the hound would soon wriggle his way into his tunic.

'You can come out,' she said, relief in her words.

'I may need some help. Jack has me pinned in,' he said with a chuckle.

'Jack,' Iona cooed sweetly, 'come get a treat, my love.' With that, he crawled out slowly with her encouragement and Royce was free to wriggle out himself. When he removed the blanket and sat up, he took a deep breath and exhaled.

'What happened?' he asked.

'I noticed five men at the start of my conversation with Chisholm and four near the end. I figured one of them had to be checking out the cottage and barn, peering in to see what he could find even after the group of them left. I was right. I saw him leave but a few minutes ago.'

'Are your neighbours always so mistrustful?'

'Aye,' she answered with a sigh in her voice. 'Not all, but some of them have long believed I am some sort of witch, despite how often those in town use my skills and services. Ridiculous nonsense, but it is hard to dispel gossip and long-held misconceptions about healers. Some used to believe the same of my mother and grandmother. Their mistrust goes both ways. I do not always trust or believe them either, especially not Chisholm. He has far too much power over the town.'

'Oh?'

'He comes from the island's wealthiest family and they have not always wielded such power with care.' That edge entered her voice again. She wasn't telling him everything, but his instinct told him to leave it be. She would tell him in time if he needed to know.

'What was that song you were singing? The tune sounded familiar, but I don't know why.' Royce walked about, placing his hands out to get his bearings. He knocked into the table and then sat back in the chair.

Iona didn't answer at first. 'A song a childhood friend of mine used to sing. Her name was Catriona. She was my best friend before Father and I moved out of town and into this cottage along the shore after my mother passed. While she would occasionally come visit me, I lost touch with her after her caregiver died and she was sent away to work for the Chisholms. I don't know what happened to her after that although I tried many a time to find out.'

'Pretty name,' he offered.

'She was a pretty girl, too.' Her voice was wistful, emotion lifting the ends of her words, so each ended softer than it began. 'Beguiling auburn-gold hair and eyes like topaz. A shade I've never seen before or since.'

'Were you the same age?'

'Aye. I think so. She was found on the shores much like you were, washed in from the sea. Her parents never found. She was raised by the kind old widow who found her and lived along the shoreline on the other side of the island until the woman died.'

Thunder boomed, rattling the small cottage once more.

'I believe she is the girl on your miniature,' she added softly. 'I am most certain of it.'

The hairs on Royce's arm stood on end, a prickle of memory itching at the back of his mind. 'What?' He began to stand, but fatigue was settling in. He clutched for the chair and sat down.

Iona gripped his shoulder. 'Are you unwell?'

'Tired...and shocked.' He sucked in a breath and closed his eyes. 'Why did you not tell me that you knew the girl in the miniature?' he demanded.

She sighed, removing her hand from his shoulder. The chair creaked as she sat down in it. 'Because it is nonsensical. How on earth would you know her? It has been over a decade.'

He stilled. 'How old are you now?'

'Almost twenty-four.'

'How old do I appear to be?' he asked, his pulse increasing at the absurdity of not knowing his age.

But there were a great deal many things he did not know any more.

Namely who he was.

'Late twenties, perhaps.'

'So, she is not my daughter.'

'Nay,' she said hesitantly.

'Why did you say she might be? Why did you lie to me?'

'I cannot say. At first, it was out of confusion. Then, out of fear.'

'Fear? Fear of what?'

'Perhaps fear over finding out she is dead and lost to me as well. Most miniatures such as this are done in memoriam and the thought of yet another loss…' She paused and then continued, her voice stronger and more resolute. 'I don't know to be sure, but fear kept me from telling you.'

'And now? Why bother telling me the truth now?'

'Because I desperately wish to know what happened to her, and…' she paused '…and I do not believe in coincidences. Something brought you to this shore, at this time, to me. I wish to know what it was and why.'

He stilled. 'You believe in fate or the like?'

'I do.'

He scoffed. 'Fate. What a farce. Then, perhaps you can tell me why fate has done such to me.'

'I cannot,' she answered softly. 'Nor will I try.'

He felt for the miniature on the table and clutched it in his hand. 'Perhaps she can,' he said bitterly as the pounding in his head began once more. He pressed his hand to his temple to dull the ache. It didn't work.

'Royce, do not plague yourself. I should not have told you. It was too soon. You have been through too much in one day.'

'Nay. I have not done enough for I cannot remember. I cannot see.'

'Your memory will return and then we will both

know the truth. Until then, you must rest. Tomorrow we will try to piece together more from what we do know.'

The woman had a point, but he would resist conceding to it despite the pounding in his head.

She rose, then returned, pressing a warm tankard into his hands. 'Have a tincture with some tea. It will aid with the fatigue and help you sleep.'

He relented and lifted the tankard to his lips and drank his fill, the warm liquid soothing as it coated his throat and warmed his belly.

'You should rest,' she offered. 'Come to the bed.'

'I will sleep on the floor,' he countered, his eyelids growing heavy. He struggled to keep them open.

'Nay.'

'Blast,' he cursed. The tincture was potent and he grew weary as his body gave in to the demand for rest.

She pulled him up by the shoulder. 'Stop your grousing and go to bed. You will feel better in the morn.' His thigh collided with the side of the mattress, and he flopped on to it, despite his best efforts to remain upright. His limbs became so heavy he struggled to move.

'Sleep well, Royce,' she murmured, her fingers feathering along his forehead like an angel's wings brushing his skin, and he sighed. 'You might even wake knowing who you are,' she added wistfully.

'I already do,' he muttered bitterly turning away from her. 'I am no one. I am merely a laird without a past.'

Chapter Seven

Iona stared down at Royce for long minutes, running her fingertips over his fine brow and cheeks. 'What secrets do you hide, my laird?' she whispered.

Probably as many as she did. She ran her other hand over the ugly, dark puckered scar along her cheek. It was in stark contrast to his fine complexion and bold features. She was grateful that he could not yet see the horror of what she was. Once he did, the threads of connection they were building would break and she would be alone once more.

Few could even bear to look upon it too long. While she had tried every balm and ointment she could, nothing worked. The cut to her face sustained on the night of the boating accident that killed her father had been too deep and the stitches poorly done. While the townsfolk had tried their best and saved her life in their efforts, her scar was hideous. She'd long learned to turn her damaged cheek away when speaking with others to make everyone more comfortable.

While she knew her fingers should not be running

along Royce's brow and the wrinkled corners at the edge of his eyes that led to his temples, she could not bring herself to stop. She'd been alone so long and his company was beginning to be something she craved like a bird longs for the dawn.

I am no one. I am merely a laird without a past.

The bitterness in his words was unmistakable and it had set her heart aflutter with guilt. She'd brought him back to the land of the living, yet wondered if she'd done right by him.

She'd always been so keen to save and rescue all those people and animals in her path over the last decade that she'd rarely thought upon whether it was the right and just thing to do. Whether they wished to be saved at all.

Her fingers stilled and she pulled them away, settling them in her lap. He slept peacefully now, his jaw relaxed and his once-clenched hand releasing the miniature from its clutches. She picked it up and held it to the candlelight. She studied it and then Royce. They had some similarities in their features, but not many. If they had been siblings, surely there would be a stronger physical connection between them.

A lost love?

She frowned. Nay. He would have a more recent portrait. One of her as a woman, not a child. And why did he have a brooch of her? Surely, a man would have a miniature that could be carried in a pocket or on a chain instead. None of it made any sense.

Perhaps she should just enjoy Royce's company for the time he was here and not worry so about everything else along the way. The answers with him and his connection with Catriona would be revealed. She just needed to be patient and not fret over all she could not control right now.

Worry is only worry, my little fish. It changes nothing and merely steals your smile.

'You are right as always, Papa,' she whispered. She rose from the bed and readied herself and her own sleeping arrangements by the fire. To her surprise, Jack jumped from the bed and curled into her side, resting his head along the slope of her hip. The storm raged, but they were all safe within. A hermit, a rescue and a blind man all tucked in for the eve. The oddity of the situation brought a smile to her lips. What her father would say if he could see her now. Strangely, she believed he would approve, even if she was sharing a cottage with a strange man she did not know.

Iona was drifting in the mystical place between wakefulness and sleep when a shout snatched her back into the present. She bolted up and glanced around. Royce shouted again and flailed on the mattress. Jack rose and trotted over to him, watchful and uncertain, before releasing a solitary bark. Iona stood and went to Royce, her blanket haphazardly wrapped around her shoulders. When she remembered he could see nothing, she shrugged it off. She could be stark naked and the man would be none the wiser.

Kneeling by the bed, she reached out to shake his shoulder, hoping the gentle action would be enough

to pull him back from his dream. She shook his arm
once and then twice, but he did not wake and shouted
again. This time it was a name. 'Violet!'

'Royce?' Iona said louder, gripping his tunic.

He turned and clutched her to him. She stilled in
his fierce grip.

He sat up, his eyes wide and unseeing. 'Violet?'
he said once more.

'Nay,' Iona replied. ''Tis me. Iona. You were dreaming. You are in my cottage. On Lismore. Do you remember?'

His eyes blinked and his shoulders drooped in relief.

'It did not feel like a dream. It felt as real as you
feel in my hold now,' he answered in ragged breaths,
still gripping her arms. He gazed behind her, his features pinched and brow furrowed.

'You cried out. I came to wake you,' she murmured,
trying to console him. The warm feel of his hands on
her and the proximity of his body to her own should
have bothered her, but it didn't.

'My apologies,' he added, dropping his hands as
if her limbs were hot cinders in his palms.

'No need. It is I who came to you.' She shifted
away from him. He threw off the blanket and flopped
back on the bed, covering his eyes with his forearm.
His chest rose and fell irregularly.

She sat silently with him as his breathing began to
return to normal. Then she risked an enquiry as the
storm still raged outside.

'Did you remember something?'

He stilled and pulled his forearm from his face. 'I remembered a girl. Violet. I was chasing after her, but she was pulled out to sea. I was but a boy and not fast enough or strong enough to save her. She was so small and the sea so large.' He shivered.

Iona leaned forward, eager to know more. Lightning lit up the room soon followed by thunder. Jack jumped on the mattress and nudged his nose under Royce's arm. He absently ran his hand down the dog's coat.

'I think…' he said and then paused. 'I believe she was my sister. And she looked exactly as you describe your friend Catriona to be, but that was not her name.' He shook his head. 'I think my mind and memories are scrambled and trying to sort out the present from the past. So am I.'

'It has been but a day since you have even awakened. It will take time, which thankfully we have much of.'

'Do you suppose I have a sister? Or other siblings?' he asked.

'If you are indeed a laird, then, aye, I think you do.'

'What of you? Do you have any brothers or sisters?'

'Nay,' she answered simply. 'Perhaps I would have if my mother had not died when I was so young, or if Father had ever remarried, but he did not. He could never overcome losing her.' That familiar longing to have had siblings of her own budded up, knocking against her ribs and feeling hollow. She wrung her hands in her lap.

'You would have been a fine older sister,' he said.

'And you could still be a mother, clucking over her babes as you have over me.'

She bit her lip and rose from the bed, removing herself from such talk. Perhaps she had longed for a family at one time, but after the boating accident, she'd set aside such longings. Her face being too scarred and her fear of losing yet another person she loved thrust her into further solitude and isolation.

It was far safer to be alone.

'Would you like me to make you another tincture?' she asked.

'Nay. I don't wish to have another dream such as that one. Is it morn yet?'

'Not for another hour.'

His stomach growled long and low.

She chuckled. 'But I can put on some oats for you. Your stomach seems to believe otherwise.'

'Aye. Thank you. What can I do to help? My hands and body grow restless for work and movement. Having a task may also help to ease my mind, which is spinning.'

'Do you know how to peel vegetables?' she asked, anticipating the answer. A laird would have little experience in such things. She put the pot of oats over the fire in the hearth and wiped her hands down her shift and shivered, realising she needed to put on some actual clothes, whether he could see her or not.

'Nay,' he said. 'But I can learn.'

'Do you wish to?' she asked.

He shrugged. 'Wish might be a strong word, but I would like to help.'

'Then we will peel vegetables for our stew later as the oats cook. Give me but a minute.'

Iona opened the cottage door and let Jack out before heading to her small wardrobe to pick out a dress for the day. She paused briefly and glanced back at Royce. Then she slid the shift off her body and stood naked before him. The idea of being completely exposed to him, but him seeing nothing, was exhilarating and enticing all at the same time. She faced him and watched him staring blankly out before him in her direction, yet seeing nothing.

What would you think of me if you could see me right now? Would you still think I was beautiful? Like you did that first night?

Or would he see her as she was? A gruesome scarred creature deserving of sympathy, but little else. Her cheeks heated and she yanked on her grey morning dress, securing the button at the top before pulling her hair out from the collar. She brushed out her long, dark tresses and bound them up in a tidy knot at the nape of her neck as she did every day. She would do well to remember that he would be gone soon and she was no heroine to be rescued.

She already had everything she needed, didn't she?

'Iona?' Royce called. 'Are you still there?'

'Aye,' she answered. 'I was just changing.'

'Just now?' The mattress creaked as he shifted his weight.

She stilled. 'Aye. I did not think it would matter for you cannot see me.'

He cleared his throat. 'I suppose not. Although it does leave ample room for the imagination.'

'Does it bother you?'

'Nay, but do not tell me next time.'

'Why ever not?'

'Well, I am blind, but I am not dead. And I am a man.'

'I will keep that in mind.'

A pawing sounded at the door and Royce clambered up.

''Tis just Jack. He wants back in,' Iona offered and let her beloved hound back inside. She grabbed her cloak from its hook near the door. 'I must check on the animals,' she said. 'I will return to show you how to peel those many vegetables.'

As she closed the door, she paused taking deep full breaths of the air, still heavy with moisture. It was dark, windy and full of chill, but she felt so alive. Far more alive than she had felt in years. Was it solely because of Royce? Was it because she felt needed? Desired even? She shrugged. It didn't matter.

What mattered was that she was almost…happy.

She went about her ablutions and then travelled to the barn to check on the animals and ensure they were still secure, despite their restlessness from the storm that was casting about bolts of lightning and thunder that shook the ground.

As she secured the final latch on the hen house, a crash sounded in the cottage, followed by a bark from Jack. Holding her cloak in place around her head as the wind and rain raged, she rushed back to the cottage. Who knew what the man had done? She prayed he had not injured himself.

Once inside, she knew exactly what had happened. The pot full of oats was on the floor, half of its contents being lapped up by Jack, as Royce clutched his hand and cursed.

'Did you burn yourself?' she asked.

'Aye,' he confessed. She touched his burned hand and he winced. 'In my attempt to help, I have created another disaster for you to attend to. My apologies.'

'Well, Jack is much pleased with your efforts as he is enjoying half a pot of cooked oats. Aren't you, my boy?'

Royce almost smiled at that. 'I'm glad one of us is benefitting.'

'There is still enough for us left in the pot. No harm done.' She would not tell him those were the last of their oats. It did not matter when they were cast about on the floor. She would just eat a smaller portion to ensure he had enough. He would be none the wiser.

'What happened?'

'I thought to help by bringing the oats back to the table. I could not find a rag to use to hold the handle of it, so I tried to use the sleeve of my tunic.'

'And how did your tunic fare?' she asked, peeking down at his sleeve, which appeared singed. 'Ah, as I suspected. Not well.'

He sucked in a breath as she tested the skin on his hand, to see how it reacted to her touch.

'I don't think you will get a boil from it, so that is

good news. We will still wrap it with some herbs to keep the swelling and pain down as much as we can.'

'So much for assisting you.'

'You will. Just not now. Why don't you step out, take care of your needs and, when you return, I will have your tincture ready and we can break our fast.'

He nodded.

'Do you remember how many steps to the out-house?

'Aye. I will manage.'

She wasn't as confident, but she did not say as much. She wanted him to know someone believed in him. 'Call out if you need me,' she added as he stepped outside. She hadn't been able to suppress that last tiny offer of help before he left.

When he returned, most of the remnants of the spill had been cleaned up and two steaming bowls of oats sat on the wooden table ready to be consumed. As he approached, she could see something was troubling him. A deep V creased his brow and a frown tugged down the corner of his lips. He did not join her at the table, but stood in the middle of the cottage frozen. Lightning flashed, illuminating his profile. He looked every bit the handsome, seasoned warrior and laird she believed he was. Then she noticed the mud splattered on his trews and up one sleeve of his tunic. He must have fallen.

'I cannot do this,' he said, frustration clipping his words, making them tight angry syllables cutting through the air like daggers. 'I am a burden to you. I will be a burden to everyone. I will not learn. I cannot help you. I cannot even manage to go to the out-house on my own without falling.'

'While that may be true now, it does not mean it will be that way for ever. Allow yourself time to learn. Give yourself the gift of patience. Grant yourself some grace.'

'Why?' he asked bitterly. 'Why do you bother with a man like me? Surely there are far better animals in need of healing and redemption than me. I thought of walking straight into the water after I fell and allowing the sea to take me for good…to save you and whatever family awaits me the burden of caring for me.'

The anguish in his voice threatened to drown out the thundering of her heart.

'What stopped you?' she asked calmly. Her words cut against the quiet crackling of the fire inside and the raging winds and rain outdoors. 'There is a storm. You could have walked easily into the water and I never would have seen you again. You would have been pulled out to sea and that would have been the last of you. Is that not your wish?' she challenged as she stepped closer to him. Her anger and frustration matched his anguish. She had known a man just like him. A man so broken by loss that he could barely care for himself, let alone a daughter.

Her father.

Royce's mouth gaped open and then closed. His Adam's apple bobbed in his throat as if the emotion of what she said and what he felt fought against one another to get out. He clenched his hands and fists at his sides.

'So? What stopped you?' she asked again. 'I brought you back to life and I have a right to know. Do I not?'

'You,' he said angrily, the word so accusatory and staccato that it landed on her as painfully as it seemed it was for him to even say.

'Me?' she replied. Of all the things she thought he might say, it wasn't that. She'd never been anyone's reason for anything. Had she?

'Aye,' he replied shifting on his feet. 'After I fell, I clambered up in frustration and all I could think of was walking into the water to make all of this…' he shook his hands out around him '…go away. But with every step I heard you in my head telling me not to give up. And the closer I got to the water the heavier my body felt, as if I was having to bring you along with me into those waters. As if by drowning myself… I was also drowning you.'

His words left her speechless. She gaped back at him, mirroring his own awestruck features. She took one quiet step towards him and then another. The air between them was charged in a way she had never felt before. Her fingers tingled with the urge and the need to touch him although she had no right to. He was not hers.

'Well,' she whispered, a mere step away from him. She was so close that he could easily seize her and she him, but she didn't. 'It is a good thing,' she continued, 'that I am well versed in dealing with a proud stubborn man like you who does not wish to be saved and who does not know the gifts they have to still share with the world.'

'And it is a better thing,' he said, reaching out his hand to skim along the fabric of the sleeve of her dress, 'that I am the gentleman that I am.' His arm fell away. 'Otherwise,' he said, pausing to swallow, 'I might very well act upon the thoughts in my head as they relate to you. I know you are no witch…but you bewitch me all the same.'

Gooseflesh pebbled her skin as if she had come out of the water into the chill of the air. His words were thick with meaning and her own imagination bloomed with all the ideas surrounding the intention of his words. 'And if I wanted you to?'

He sucked in a breath and stepped back. Releasing an uneasy laugh, he felt for the back of the chair before he sat down. 'Even though I cannot see, I know that you are a far finer creature than should be allowed to be touched by a man like me.'

He picked up the bowl of steaming oats and guided the lip of it gently to his mouth before eating his fill. She stared back at him, wondering what it would feel like to have those lips of his on hers and whether he would believe her to be so fair and fine a creature if he could see her for himself.

Chapter Eight

Royce had never given the idea of purgatory much thought until now when he was trapped in a small cottage with a woman as soft and supple as Iona, who smelled of hope and whom he dared not touch. The small incremental sufferings of self-control wedged so finely against desire and wholeness could scarce be borne, but he would have to endure it.

He could not leave this little isle without knowing the truth of who had tried to kill him and why he'd even come. Nor could he act upon his base desire to claim the woman who had saved him, the woman who cared about his well-being and life more than he did, as his own. What little he knew of himself, he at least knew this: he was no cad and he was no rakehell, but, unfortunately, he was still a man.

A man weak of the flesh, but strong in the mind. The world was a mind-numbing duality with Iona MacKenzie in it.

Even now as he set down the bowl of oats on the table he knew where she was by the smell of the air near him. He could also hear her subtle footfalls to the table and her sliding into the chair, the rush of fabric against the wood. The shift in weight against the table leg, a small jostling of sorts. Had he frightened her with what he'd said? He hadn't meant to. He just didn't know how else to get her to step away from him, how else to break the crushing pull between them as they'd stood there arguing over the worth of his life.

'Are you not hungry?' he asked. She hadn't moved since she'd joined him at the table.

'Nay.'

He didn't have to ask the cause of her losing her appetite. His behaviour had most surely caused it. 'You must eat.'

'As you must live?' she asked.

He smiled. 'Aye. As I must live.'

'Then, I will eat,' she replied. A spoon scraped against the wooden bowl and his shoulders relaxed in relief. She was his tether to this world and without her he did not know what he would do. Yet another reason he could not act upon his attraction and fracture the precarious nature of their arrangement.

'What shall you do today?' he asked. 'And how can I make myself useful?'

'I must catch up with making my tinctures, but I also need to tend to the animals and any clean up from the storm.'

'Perhaps tinctures first? Then I can try to help you with clean up?'

'It will be too great a risk to have you out of doors

as the men from town may be about checking upon the welfare of the shoreline and still looking for you, but I can set you to some tasks within the cottage.'

His shoulders slumped. He had forgotten about the risk of being out of doors and the nosy neighbours who threatened his safety. Assisting her would be far more difficult than he realised.

Iona rose and gathered the used bowls and spoons from the table. 'Now that I think about it, I will set you to grinding up the herbs. You are strong and it is a sedentary task which takes much time. While you are grinding up the ingredients with a mortar and pestle, I can be outside checking on the animals, feeding them, and cleaning up any storm debris.

While the task would not prove exciting, at least he would be helping. 'What shall I make first?' he asked, eager to do something to busy his hands and tidy up his idle mind.

'We shall make the two orders for megrim powders. They're one of my top requests and I find I'm quite good at making them after all these years.'

'Megrim powders it is,' he replied.

'Stay there. I will bring them to you.'

She bustled around the small cottage. He focused on what he could hear and imagined the movements with it. Canisters were gathered about and set on the table with one small thud after another. Then, a stone mortar and pestle were placed before him and his hands brought to it. The shock from sliding from Iona's warm hands to the cool stone was jolting.

'Here,' she whispered, taking his hand and wrapping it around the pestle. 'Grind this down until I return. Use firm, controlled, twisting motions,' she added as she guided his hand with the movement she wished for him to mimic.

The combination of the sweet, heated pressure from her fingers on his own and the wispy brush of a loose strand of her hair along his neck sent fire through him, and he commanded himself to listen to her instruction. 'The finer the powder the better for the mixture. I will see to the animals.'

'Aye,' he answered, releasing a breath of relief after she moved away. He began the repetitive twisting motion to crush whatever herbs she had added to the mortar into a fine powder.

Royce found the repetitive motion oddly soothing, much like he did when he stroked Jack's fur. Another flash of memory overcame him: the smooth rhythmic sliding back and forth of a blade against a whetstone to sharpen it. The more he ground down the powder with his pestle, the clearer the memory became.

He was guiding his own blade against a whetstone over and over in a large armory all alone. No noise or people were around. He stilled as he heard footsteps and the voice of a young woman.

'Couldn't you have a soldier or servant do that for you?' the woman asked. Although she looked familiar, she had no name.

Royce ceased his movements, glanced at her, then continued the steady, recurrent strokes of the metal against stone. 'I prefer to not trust anyone else to sharpen my blades.'

'Royce?' Another female voice snatched him back to the present.

Reluctantly, he blinked and sucked in a breath. Remembering fatigued him and weariness washed over him.

'Royce?'

It was Iona's voice. Not the other female voice from his memories.

'I was in an armoury sharpening a dagger,' he sputtered out. 'There was a woman who came to see me, but I know not who she was although she seemed familiar.'

'Was it Catriona? Or the girl you remembered named Violet?'

'Nay,' he replied, shaking his head. 'I don't think so, but it came and went from my mind so quickly.' He rubbed a hand through his hair. 'Too quickly.'

'But you are remembering,' Iona replied. 'That is fine news.' She rested her hand on his shoulder. 'It means your memory will return in time.'

He only hoped he liked what he remembered. The knot in his stomach made him uncertain, but he didn't wish to counter the excitement in Iona's voice.

In his memory, he was hard. Angry. Much like he had been with Iona. He hadn't liked himself when he'd done it. Would he like the man he was?

If he didn't, could he change it?

'The animals fared well,' she told him. 'I will bring in some fresh goat's milk in a few minutes. You did well with the grinding,' she added, taking the mortar from him. 'Here is more to be ground down.'

He clutched the pestle and began anew, hoping returning to the movements of before would thrust him back into the same memory. Minutes ticked by, but the memory did not return.

It was replaced by doubt.

How long would it take for him to remember? How long would it take for him to discover who had tried to have him killed or why he came to the isle at all?

The door opened and closed. He stopped grinding.

Iona paused near him, her floral scent now mixed with earth and animal from being in the barn. He smiled, as he found he didn't mind it.

'This arrangement may serve us well,' she said. 'As I work, you do as well and twice the tasks have been accomplished.' She took the mortar from him again. 'Your reward for your efforts,' she said, pushing a tankard into his hand. 'Drink.'

And he did. The goat's milk was sweet and hearty and he drained the cup, savouring it.

'Could you do one more while I gather up some wood for the hearth?'

'Of course,' he said. 'I have done little while you have done much.'

'Your strength is a blessing. It takes me much longer to grind down the herbs, so I am grateful for your help.' She set another mortar full of herbs before him. 'I will return.'

As he set to the task again, he took in the simplicity of the life he had here versus what he expected might be a very complicated life as laird. What challenges did he face? Were his people safe even though he had disappeared? Surely he did have siblings as Iona said to take the lead in his absence.

He stilled. Perhaps they even relished his absence and would spend little if any time in search of him, being none too eager for his return.

The thought chilled him, so he cast it aside as quickly as he'd thought it.

The day had spun out like a fine tapestry of work, talk and rest. He'd napped twice by the eve, which he could hardly fathom, but he tired easily. While he hated his weakness, nothing could be done but accept it and surrender to his body's demand for sleep. He'd wake, feeling rested, and return to the next task Iona set before him.

'It shall be dark soon,' she stated later that afternoon. 'Once it is I shall deliver the tinctures to the proper homes and go for a swim. It has been two nights since my last and my body craves the sea.'

'Swim?' he sputtered. 'At night?'

'Aye. It is how I found you, remember?'

'I had forgotten. Is it truly safe? You could be harmed by debris, boats and whatever else enjoys the cool waters.'

'Nay,' she countered. 'I have been swimming since I was a very small child. My father's nickname for me was Little Fish because I loved the water so.'

'Little Fish, eh?' He nodded. 'I suppose that does suit.'

Chapter Nine

Iona's breath caught, her chest and throat tightening with emotion.

No one had called her that in such a long time.

To hear Royce use her father's nickname for her filled her heart, but why? She barely knew the man and he hardly even knew himself. Yet she had told him things about herself that she had not shared in a long time, if ever. Every morsel of her past she shared with him made the memories feel brighter within her, as if him knowing them made them less likely to disappear and be forgotten for ever.

'When shall you return?' he asked, a hint of worry in his words.

'As soon as I can. Jack shall keep you company instead of coming with me. That way I will not worry about what you are up to and he can alert you to any people who may come this way. Please stay inside while I am gone to ensure your safety.'

'And who shall care for you? Travelling at night with no protection? Swimming in the dark waters of the loch by moonlight alone? I do not think it wise.' His voice held censure, but she steered around it, knowing full well worry drove his words.

'I have been alone long before your arrival and I shall continue to be after you are gone. I will protect myself. It is one of the many things I have grown accustomed to and I find that, like healing, I am quite good at it. I have had much practice.' She put on her cloak and tied the ribbon to secure it at her throat.

'Take my dagger,' he offered.

'I am afraid you do not have one to offer. It was scavenged before I reached you.'

'Bloody hell,' he groused. 'Is nothing sacred? To steal my blade off me?'

'In their defence, they believed you dead. From afar I did, too.' She lifted the hood over her head and began to collect the tinctures for her basket to take for delivery.

'But I was not,' he countered. 'And even still, to steal a dead man's blade is in poor taste indeed.'

'Perhaps. I do not need a weapon anyway,' she offered.

'Why not? You are a young woman traversing alone at night. You should be wary.'

'I will be,' she answered, biting her lip. She would not tell him that her scarred face and her unusual gifts as a healer made men and women alike wary enough of her to allow her a wide berth whenever she came upon anyone. Some people thought her a witch and a scarred witch at that. She'd done her part in never correcting them. It suited her desire for privacy and solitude.

Connection was full of risk and she'd lost enough to keep any possibility of such at a distance. She would do well to remember that with Royce, too.

'I still do not like it.'

'Well, do you like to eat?' she asked in exasperation.

'Aye.'

'Then this is what we must do. What I must do. To ensure we all eat.'

He said nothing, but stared blankly in her direction, gripping the back of a chair as he stood.

'Drop the latch after I leave.'

Iona heard the latch drop like a hammer to seal the cottage door closed.

Stubborn man. It was hard for him to allow her to help him. Part of her understood that, but it didn't mean she couldn't be irritated with him now, did it?

She closed her eyes and sucked in a breath of the cool night air, eager to be on her way for her deliveries and to dive headlong into the cool waters of the loch afterwards as her reward. Her muscles were tight from her lack of swimming and begged to be stretched and worked to their limits once more.

She climbed the small rolling beach, watching the stars twinkle overhead in the clear crisp midnight sky that always followed such a storm. Debris still littered some of the shoreline, but with such a storm gifts were often left by the sea. Her eyes scanned the beach line, wondering what treasures the loch had given this time. She smiled at the thought of what the sea had brought her last time: Royce.

The man was an unusual creature. Unlike any man she had known before, not that she had known that many. He was headstrong, stubborn and fiercely protective, even of her, someone he hardly knew. While she realised some of that care was based on his dependency on her due to his blindness and lack of memory, there was another part of that protection that ran far deeper. And she wanted desperately to know where it came from. Perhaps his care was brotherly? Or born out of habit from being a laird?

She clutched her basket tightly. Or could she dare risk the idea that he might care for her as she feared she might be starting to care for him? Her attraction to him was undeniable. He was something akin to a Celtic warrior she'd heard stories of as a child. But his attraction to her, if there was one, was odd indeed.

She crested the final hill and headed into town, tugging her cloak tightly around her face. While everyone knew who she was, most did not speak to her at all. Whether it be from discomfort from her scarred face or her occupation she did not know. But she did know she was invisible. And part of her liked it that way.

The other part of her was lonely, but too scared to change her life. Being seen meant being hurt, didn't it? Perhaps that was why she felt so drawn to Royce. He did not know her past and could not see her imperfections. She could be someone new to him and she'd not had anything close to a fresh start in a long time.

Or ever.

She reached her first delivery and left the small pouch of megrim medicine at the front door. She knocked softly and walked away. At a distance, she heard the door creak open and then close. Since the deliveries were close together, she completed them quickly and soon she stood staring at the haunting remains of St Moluag's Cathedral, a place of fascination for her since she was a child. Even now in the darkness, the moonlight reflected off the remnants of the stone chancel that had been here long before her and would remain long after. The partial roof revealed long shadows and mysteries of the last thousand years before her.

'Do you believe he is still here, Papa?' Iona asked, clutching her father's hand as the wind whispered around her, through her.

'Who?' he asked.

'St Moluag,' she replied.

'What do you think, Little Fish?' he whispered, kneeling beside her.

'I almost feel him in the wind,' she admitted, risking a gaze at her parents.

'I always feel him, too,' her mother replied, running a hand over Iona's hair. 'Perhaps it is the healer in you.'

'Or perhaps you were meant to spread his kindness and care, just like your mother always has.' His gaze filled with emotion. 'He sends you his strength, bravery and cunning, too. Moluag was a strong man set on saving those he could.'

'Then that is what I shall do, too, Papa,' she answered, smiling back at him.

'I would expect nothing less,' he replied, pressing a kiss to her forehead.

Iona blinked back the memory and wiped a tear from her cheek. How his words were still so true, so strangely accurate. Perhaps St Moluag had guided Royce to these shores on purpose. To save him and return him to his people. Iona continued, moving instinctively to her parents' graves, nestled side by side facing east so they could relish in the morning sunrise, their favourite time of day. She placed a single white meadowsweet bloom on each one, knowing full well her mother would chastise her for wasting one of the most sacred herbs on them, but she didn't care. Perhaps it could still relieve any pain they suffered in the other world just as it eased pain from the living. A foolish, childish thought, she knew, but she left the sprigs on their shadowy graves with a prayer just the same.

'Iona?' a man said.

She stilled, knowing full well who it was, and smiled. She rose from the graves and faced the one man who always greeted her, come wind or rain, or the time of day or season. 'Reverend,' she said. 'How are you this eve?'

'Seeking solace from the past, like you, I suppose,' he replied as he approached. He was bundled in a woollen scarf and coat, his grey hair ruffled by the light breeze. 'On my way to see Bess.' He gestured to his wife's grave, which was five headstones down from her parents'.

'Aye. The solace is brief, but always welcome,' she said. 'I have a sprig of meadowsweet left, if you'd like to add it to your own.' She offered the flower to him and he accepted it with a shaking, weathered hand.

'Thank you.' He lifted the sprig to his nose. 'One of her favourites as well as mine. You know you are always welcome,' he said, gesturing to the chapel. Every week he invited her to return to the parish she used to attend with her family. Every week she replied the same.

'I know. And I am grateful for your offer, as always. I just do not feel it best.' She gripped her basket tightly, her pulse picking up speed.

He nodded and ran his fingertips over the blooms of the meadowsweet, releasing a light, sweet fragrant scent of almonds. 'You do not have to hide yourself, my dear. There are people who care for you.'

She shifted on her feet and glanced down at them. 'I know you believe that to be true, but I do not. It is better that I stay away. People are uncomfortable around me.'

'Or perhaps you are uncomfortable around them?'

She lifted her head and met his gaze. 'That, too.'

'No matter,' he answered. 'One day you will be ready and, when that day comes, we will welcome you with open arms.'

'Thank you, Reverend.'

He nodded and walked on to see his late wife.

Iona continued her way down the hillside to the

main road to grant him the privacy he deserved. Candlelight flickered in the cottages as she passed through the area of town from the church back to the beach and imagined the families within. Were they laughing or sharing stories from the day? Sharing a late meal by the hearth? Was a woman darning a hole in a tunic or mending a pair of trews? She hugged her cloak to her body. This part of her journey was always the loneliest as she saw what she was missing as the recluse she was and had to face the knowing that such a family would never be hers.

Finally, she reached the edge of the raised beach and began the descent to her home. She checked the small, raised box on its post at the edge of the land around her cottage and found three new requests for tinctures along with their coin payments and placed them in her basket. Then she tugged off her boots, rolled down her tights and left them near her coin box.

Walking barefoot along the sand and pebbles, she let the soles of her feet grip the earth once more. She sighed from the sweet feel of Scotland beneath her toes and paused to stare out and listen to the soft rolling waters of the loch. It beckoned her.

She stripped down to her shift, tucking her neatly folded clothes on top of her coin and medicinal requests. Standing in the chill, she felt gooseflesh rise in greeting to the night air. Then she walked to the waters, waded in and dived deep into the silence and refuge that only her nightly swims offered.

The cool tranquil waters kissed her skin as her limbs cut neatly through the loch. Stroke after stroke she pulled herself further out into the depths. As her limbs tired, she slowed. She treaded water and stared out at the cottage, wondering what Royce was doing without her.

It was odd to think about the day she found him. How her daily life had changed since spying him on the beach almost a week ago. It made her wonder what the next day and week might hold for her. Would he remember who he was and leave?

Stranger still, would he remember who he was and stay?

Voices sounded across the water and she scanned the area for nearby boats. She saw none, but continued her survey, knowing full well how deceptive sound was across the loch. The men could be all the way across the water standing on land and sound as if they were behind her shoulder. Finally, she saw a lantern bobbing in the hand of a man along the shoreline on the beach north of where she lived. Three other men trailed behind him, sharing their own lantern between them. The candles within the lanterns flickered, fighting to keep their light against the quick halting movements of the men as they travelled.

'Sailor's fortune,' she cursed.

They were heading straight to the cottage. Her stomach tightened and she bit her lip. She could not swim back and get to the cottage unseen before they reached her door. She hoped that Jack would alert Royce in time for him to hide out of sight of the windows as the men passed. Surely, her home was not their real destination, but along their path to town.

She squinted. But they didn't look to be Chisholm and his men. So, who could it be?

It was far too late in the eve for fishermen. And a might bit too early for men to be heading to the inn. Not many strangers to the isle came this far north as there was little here. The leader of the men shouted to them and they quickly headed further inland from the shoreline and separated into the brush as if hunting for something they had lost in their previous travels. Soon, one man called out to them and they all came to him, huddled around something deep in the brush.

Iona's throat dried. One word she could hear above the water and decipher with ease.

Dead.

Chapter Ten

Royce paced the small cottage. While Iona had been gone, he had mapped the dimensions of the tidy space and knew exactly how many of his own steps it took to reach the hearth, the bed, the front door, the kitchen area and the small table and chairs where they ate. He scrubbed his hands down his face and rested them along his waist, staring out into the familiar dark abyss that always greeted him. What he did *not* know was when she would return. Surely hours had passed since her departure.

His body was restless and his mind spun with worries over her safety. Why did the woman traverse only at night and swim in the pitch black? It could not be safe to take such risks night after night, tempting the fates and entrusting her well-being to the sound reasoning of men and beast alike.

As much as he was loathe to admit it, he cared about this woman whom he'd only known two days. Such a confession was beyond reason, but it was the truth. While he knew part of his concern was that he was entirely dependent upon her for his well-being, the depths of his feelings reached beyond that singular purpose of survival.

Jack released a low growl and Royce stilled.

'What is it, boy?' he whispered. Gooseflesh rose along his skin. Not being able to see was infuriating, but he was starting to trust his other senses more now. He could still hear and abide by his gut instincts, so he would, and in spades.

Jack released a singular bark, followed by another growl, and Royce patted the dog's head. He grabbed a blanket and hid himself behind the bed as Iona had told him to if anyone neared the cottage before she returned. The air under the blanket warmed and he focused on the sounds around him. Soon, he heard voices and movement outside the cottage. Jack let out another series of warning barks and more sinister growls. Evidently, he didn't know or like whoever walked outside of the cottage, which made Royce even more wary.

The cottage door thudded roughly against its latch once and then again. Someone was trying to breach the door, but why?

Jack's growls and snapping jowls were louder and more sinister. Royce moved so he was ready to spring up from behind the bed if they forced entry.

'She be not here,' one man said, 'but her beast is. He's not here. No sign of 'im.'

'He has to be somewhere on this isle,' another younger man complained. 'He didn't die. I saw her pull him from the shore. Why else would she do that if he wasn't still alive? 'Tis just a matter of time until we find him.'

'Ye were so deep in yer cups, ye aren't sure what ye saw.'

'Nay. I know what I saw, no matter how much I had to drink. She came out of the water like a sea nymph and then later she lugged him up the shore to here. I know it.'

'Seems a fanciful tale spun to save your hide, boy,' the man spat out. 'Waste of my time coming out here. No wee lass could have dragged a man of his size inside.'

'Well, she be no ordinary woman, sir. She's a witch and everyone says so. And ye should see her scarred face. Lives out here alone to hide from everyone. Has for as long as I can remember.'

A witch? And scarring? What scarring?

'I know not why she lives way out here, nor do I care. I don't know why anyone would be living on this tiny isle. I just came here to finish the job I was hired to do and that's to kill the Laird before he figures out what his dear father did all those years ago. If I don't succeed, we'll both be dead. Webster is none too pleased with our missteps at leaving him alive. It is a miracle we are not already dead and that we have another chance to correct our mistake.'

'I…I'll find him…find proof that I am right,' the younger man said, his voice laced with ire and fear, a dangerous combination.

A combination that would put him and Iona in grave danger.

'Yer damn right ye will,' the other man said. There was a thud against the cottage wall, which sent Jack into another brief frenzy of barking and growling. 'Ye will also be buying me a drink at the inn after such a waste of my eve.'

The other man coughed. 'Aye,' he said weakly as if recovering from a sound blow to the gut.

Silence followed.

Royce's heart hammered in his chest, his pulse raging over their words. His mind spun with what he'd learned. Someone had hired men to kill him? Why? And what secrets did his father have that they were so determined to protect? Had he ever known what those secrets were? And Webster…the name sounded familiar, but why? If only his mind could right itself and sort through the past and present and weave them back together.

His gut twisted. And then there was Iona. Was it true that she was a witch, scarred and hiding in solitude perhaps in part because of it? He couldn't imagine such to be true. She was a sweet lass and gifted healer who sacrificed what little she had to care for him, risking financial and social ruin. But, why hadn't she told him? He chided himself. They had known each other two days. Of course, there was a great deal he did not know of her, but he couldn't help but wonder what secrets she was hiding from him? Could it be that she had even more secrets than he, a man who could not remember his past?

Jack nuzzled his snout against Royce's arm through the blanket. 'One more minute,' Royce whispered to the hound. He had to be sure the men were gone before he came out from behind the bed, although he felt ridiculous hiding.

He was a grown man and warrior from what Iona could surmise from the scars along his body, but he had promised her he wouldn't risk exposure for both of their sakes, and his word seemed important to him, as if it was truly all he had. Or perhaps it was part of who he was, like the tribal bands she told him were inked along his bicep. Although he didn't know what he'd lost to mark himself with such remembrances, he needed to honour what he could, which right now was his word to her.

Jack whined.

'And you,' he said, pulling the blanket off himself and taking in some fresh air. 'You did good,' he told the dog. 'You have earned more than your keep this eve.' Royce petted the dog gently and was rewarded with some licks to his cheek.

He stood and stretched his limbs. Walking over to the hearth, he held out his hands to it. The flames had long gone out as no more heat emanated from it. He felt about for wood and found it stacked neatly atop some shards of kindling he found near the fire poker. At least it would be ready to light upon her return.

He didn't wish to risk discovery by lighting it now or waste her fuel on warming the cottage just for him and Jack. No doubt she'd be freezing upon her return after swimming in the loch at night. He picked up a smaller piece of wood, driftwood by the weight of it, and found a small blade near the mantel. It had to be a woman's knife based on the small dainty grip, but it would do.

He guided the blade against the wood and it easily gave way. While he didn't know what he would make from it, such carving eased his mind and helped him think. Now that he knew someone meant him harm and by extension Iona for caring for him, he needed to devise a plan. While he was blind and had no memory, he could still think, and scheme he would.

After a while Jack rose quietly and padded over to the door. He whined and pawed at it, wanting to be let out. Royce frowned. What should he do? Was he endangering them by letting Jack out? Before he could think further on it, a soft knock sounded.

'Royce, are you awake?' Iona asked.

He smiled in relief at her being safe and in being saved from his quandary of whether to open the door or not. He rose, lifted the latch, and opened the door. He could smell the sea on her and feel the cool water dripping from her hair on his arm as she brushed past him to come inside. She greeted Jack, who whined at her before she set him outside.

'How did you fare?' she asked, closing the door. 'I hope I was not gone too long.'

'We had company,' he answered.

'Aye. I thought so. I saw them from the water as I swam.'

'Men came by. Two of them from what I could hear.

Jack alerted me to them before they reached the door, so I could be out of sight.'

'Did they sound familiar? Like the men who came before with Chisholm?' She rustled about and he stilled as he swore she was changing in front of him again. The sound of fabric rushing along her skin was becoming unnerving as he could not hear it without imagining her bare flesh inches from him.

He cleared his throat and shifted on his feet before answering, 'Nay. I did not recognise their voices. They were looking for me. I am sure of it.'

Any movements ceased. 'What?'

'You heard me. Said they were looking for the Laird. They had been tasked to kill me, it seemed, but they had failed and were eager to rectify that with my death. They also suspect you dragged me in and saved me.'

She cursed and Royce lifted his brow, trying not to smirk. A flash of memory seized him and he grabbed the back of the chair as his mind pulled him to another time and place in the past.

'Sister, Father will be none too pleased to hear you using such language.'

'You know he would not be surprised and his displeasure is a regular occurrence, is it not? Why am I not allowed to be displeased and be angry at him? He has set this impossible course for me and I hate it. Why can I not be allowed to choose my husband as you will one day be allowed to choose your wife?' she argued, her long dark plait swishing to one side

as she turned and paced away from him. 'I am daughter of the Laird. That should count for something.'

She faced him, setting her teary, bright, cool blue eyes upon him. The pain in her glare shot through him like an arrow.

'I cannot spare you his decision, no matter my thoughts,' he said evenly, trying to console her.

'That is not true. You just do not dare stand up to him.'

Anger heated his skin. 'Nay. I do not stand up to him because I agree with him on this count. You cannot marry a soldier, Susanna. It matters not how fine a soldier he may be. You are destined to marry a laird and nothing less. It is your duty to the clan.'

His words were forceful and harsh, and he knew it. But his sister had to accept the truth. She had no choice for a husband. Better she set hopes for a love match aside, just like he would.

'Says the man who shows no emotion and has no feeling.' She rushed to him, gripped his tunic and tugged on it. 'Even now,' she cried out with tears streaming down her face, 'when I am crumbling at your feet, begging for your help, you stand stoic and unyielding. You have no heart, Royce. None.'

'I will marry the woman who promises the most for the clan as well, Sister,' he answered angrily, trapping her hand in his own and pulling it away from his tunic. 'Love will have no impact on my choice. It is a sacrifice we must all make, even you.'

He stormed out to the sound of her sobs.

Royce sucked in a breath, clutching the solid wood

of the chair for balance as the memory fled him as quickly as it had come.

'Royce?' Iona called. 'What has happened?' She was by his side now and had her hand over his own as he gripped the chair fiercely, willing his pulse to slow and his breathing to become more regular.

'I had another memory,' he answered, his throat tight.

'I believe I may have two sisters,' he said wistfully.

'Was one of them Catriona?' she asked quickly.

He shook his head. 'Nay. This lass looked nothing like Catriona, nor was she like the young Violet I remembered in my dream. Her features were different. She had dark hair, these bright blue eyes and her name was Susanna.' His chest tightened at the knowing he officially had a sibling. While he was not certain of Violet, there was no mistaking Susanna was kin. He smiled. 'She had a nasty temper.'

Iona squeezed his hand and laughed. 'Perhaps that is a family trait,' she teased.

'Maybe. Although I do not think mine as bad as hers. And she called me Royce. It must be my given name.'

'Any chance she told you your surname, too?'

'Nay. But it is nice to remember and know that I have a family somewhere and that perhaps they are looking for me.'

Iona's hand slipped away and she did not answer. *Blast.*

Royce winced. Why had he said that to her? She

had no family. 'I am sorry. I was not trying to be cruel. I was not thinking.'

'Do not be foolish,' she replied. 'It is a fine thing to have family and I would never begrudge you from celebrating your memories. It means someone is looking for you and you may soon be able to return home. I am happy for you. That is what I want for you. To find your home, your memory and your family.'

And it was what he wanted for her, too. But how could he give her back a family she had already lost?

He couldn't.

'What else can you remember?'

'She was angry. Angry about not being able to marry the man she loved. I think Father had forbidden it and I…'

'You what?'

'I supported him and told her it was her duty to marry another. Just as that same duty was mine. That we were not to expect a love match as children of a laird.'

'Oh. That explains her anger quite well. She had a broken heart.'

'She said *I* had no heart.'

'Ouch. Harsh words to hear, even if from a memory.'

'Aye. But I am grateful to have had it. I have more pieces to the puzzle of who I am.'

Silence stretched out between them and Royce filled it first, uncomfortable with the thought that his sister's words might have been true. That perhaps he had no heart, that he was an unfeeling brother and an unyielding man focused solely on his responsibilities as laird.

What if the man he discovered when his memory returned was a man he did not like? He set the thought aside, unwilling to face such a possibility yet.

'And your deliveries? Your swim?' he asked, forcing himself to focus on the present.

'Fine on both accounts. I even have three more orders to fill for tomorrow, so you can get more practice with the mortar and pestle in the morn. I will light the fire and put on the stew. Gather Jack in for me?' she asked.

'Of course,' he answered and walked four steps and reached out. Although not quite at the door, he was closer than before.

'You have been practising your distances while I was away,' she praised.

'Not much else to do,' he answered, although deep down he was pleased at his progress. He opened the door and tripped over the threshold.

'Watch the—'

'Aye,' he muttered.

Oh, well. He was *almost* pleased with his progress.

'Thank you. It was delicious,' Royce said, setting down his empty bowl.

'You did a fine job of peeling the carrots and potatoes for it, so thank you as well.'

He shifted in his chair and it squeaked under his weight. 'Why do you hide here?' he said. 'Why continue to live here all alone? The men said it was because you were a witch.'

He could not add the bit about her scarring. It seemed cruel and unnecessary, even if it might be true. He would let her tell him if it was.

'Nay. Not a witch, but I do live alone as you well know. At first, it was to grieve my mother. Then, when my father died, I found I couldn't leave. As if leaving here was leaving them both behind. I have so many memories here on this island. And sometimes in the night, I visit those places we used to go just to be with them. 'Tis foolhardy, I know.'

'Nay. Just a way to remember them. I have found memories are to be cherished.'

'Aye,' she replied. 'I imagine you might know a bit about the importance of memories.'

He heard that smile again in her voice and he couldn't help but smile back.

'I will wash, if you will dry, my laird,' she chided him.

'Of course, my lady. Hand me a towel and I will be at your bidding.'

A towel snapped and zinged him in the thigh. 'Ouch,' he complained. She zinged him again. 'Not fair.'

'You are right,' she replied. 'Here is your towel.' She hit her mark once more. This time on the back of the thigh.

'Have you forgotten I am blind?'

'Nay,' she answered, landing another hit to his calf. 'But I do believe this will help you to tune into your senses. Do you not agree?'

'I do not agree,' he complained. He recovered a towel by his bowl, wound it up and whipped it out, but it snapped in the air, missing its mark.

She snapped her towel again, striking his forearm.

'Ah, you are close,' he teased. 'I can smell you.'

'Smell me?'

'Aye. A hint of the sea, but also something floral, sweet.' He released the towel into the air and she squealed.

'Just missed,' she exclaimed victoriously.

He focused on the sound of her voice and hit his mark. She yipped. 'Ouch. You are a quick study. I always thought you were a warrior despite your title.'

'Perhaps I am both,' he said, listening to her movements. There was a small creak in the floorboards that he knew came from a loose board near the hearth. He snapped his towel in that direction and landed his hit.

'Ow! But I cannot be angry. You are doing well. Quite well,' she murmured, her voice sounding closer. Royce heard the whoosh of the towel in the air and seized it, tugging her to him.

She laughed in surprise as he hauled her to him, her soft body colliding hard into his chest. Her hair was still damp from her swim. Loose strands skimmed his neck and throat as she gripped his arms.

'I fear…' she said, 'that my lesson has worked against me.'

He disagreed. He liked her lesson just fine. Her warm body next to his, her head tucked under his chin, as if that was exactly where it was supposed to be. He lifted his right hand to her cheek, wanting to know if she was as scarred as the men said, if something so beautiful in his mind had been ravaged. But all he found was smooth, delicious supple skin which heated under his palm. Her breath hitched. His caress affected her as much as it did him.

'Describe yourself to me, Iona. I want to imagine you…properly,' he said quietly.

'What is it you believe I look like, my laird? Tell me.'

Royce sucked in a breath. What was he doing? He should have let her go. He didn't know what life he had elsewhere and who else was in it, but he held her, his need for her now outweighing how temporary anything they shared might be. He cleared his throat.

'I believe you are petite, but strong from all your chores and daily labours with dark hair like the night sky, long from what I can tell. But your eyes, I am not certain of those. Blue or green, perhaps? With a strong chin full of defiance, a pert nose full of interest and perhaps a coy dimple in your cheek. Am I right on any of those counts?' he teased, trying to lighten the attraction coursing through his body and his desire to kiss her.

'Well, on some counts. I possess dark hair, a strong chin and a pert nose, but no dimples and my eyes are a mossy green. My father used to say they were the colour of the meadows in spring.'

'Just as I suspected,' he murmured in her hair.

'What is that?'

'You are far more beautiful than you should be.

Those men I overheard said you were scarred, disfigured, but they are wrong. Foolish men to be sure.'

She stiffened in his hold and stepped out of his embrace. 'Is that what they said?'

'Aye.'

'And you wished to find out for yourself rather than merely ask me?'

He was puzzled by her anger. 'I did not believe it to be true. I did not wish to hurt you by asking such.'

'And if I was? Would you have run from this cottage afeared that I was truly a witch?'

He paused. He was missing something deeply important to her, but what? Had he not just complimented her on her beauty, held her in his arms because of his attraction to her?

'Wait,' he stated. 'I do not understand. Why are you angry? If isn't true, why does it matter? I am not daft, but I do not—'

'Aye. You are daft. I will leave you to the dishes. I must tend the animals.'

'Iona?' he called after her, but with a slam of the cottage door she was gone.

Chapter Eleven

Iona rushed out to the barn, eager to escape the confines of the cottage as well as Royce. It didn't matter that it was pitch dark and she could hardly see one foot in front of the other. She would tend to the animals as she always did and pretend his actions had not hurt her. What other option was there? She could not exactly tell him *why* she was so angry.

The truth was it frightened her that he would know how ugly and disfigured her face truly was. Having him believe that she was beautiful made her feel cherished and connected to him, something she hadn't had in so long. Of course, she knew it wouldn't last, but it hadn't mattered.

He was never going to stay, so she had coveted their bit of time together. She had begun to feel true friendship and something a touch beyond that—a connection and attraction she'd never had before and one she felt protective of as if it were a new bud of a rare herb that needed to be nurtured and cherished from the raging winds and rain.

Should she have confessed the men told the truth and end the charade of pretending she was something other than the scarred witch of the sea? She could have. It would have been easy. All she had needed to do was turn her face and guide his hand to her scarred cheek. No words would have even been necessary. But she had been desperate to keep up the farce and not break the illusion of what could have been if she were the beautiful woman he imagined her to be.

Perhaps that was what she was most angry about—that he had almost shattered the lovely illusion she had created of who they were with his probing questions. She grabbed a rake and began the process of mucking out the stalls for her wee goats and chickens. Soon, her arms ached from the work, but it served as a heady distraction from the ache in her heart. After she finished scattering out the new hay, she took a deep breath and headed back in the cottage.

Candlelight flickered from a single torch on the wall and the fire languished in the hearth, dwindling down to almost nothing. All the dishes from supper as well as the pot for the stew had been cleaned and placed exactly where she would have put them. A small sprig of meadowsweet rested in her mother's vase on the kitchen table.

The care that he had taken in setting her cottage to rights made her heart skitter in her chest. In just a couple days, he had learned how to navigate the world, her world, without sight. He had also learned to cope with not knowing who he really was or the life that he had lost.

She felt as small as a dandelion seed for how she had just treated him. Her shoulders slumped. She needed to apologise.

'I tried my best to put everything back as you would like,' he said from where he sat at the small table. 'I am not entirely sure what I have done to upset you, but I am sorry. You have risked all to help me and heal me. I am grateful. Without you I would be dead. There can be no doubt about that.'

Her eyes filled and she wrung her hands, overwhelmed by his honesty and kindness. 'It looks lovely. Thank you. I am sorry for my words.'

This was her opportunity. She could share all her secrets and unburden herself. He sat at the table, staring in her general direction, waiting. There was no smile on his lips, but only concern in his wrinkled brow. She came to the table and sat across from him, letting her hand slide halfway between the two of them, but not daring to reach further.

'I went to visit my parents this eve,' she said. 'I left one of those very flowers you placed in the vase on each of their graves. Meadowsweet was always their favourite.'

He listened, sliding his palm towards hers, a whisper away from touching her own.

'They are buried outside of St Moluag's parish in town. It is a gorgeous medieval church, or at least the ruins of it are. I remember going there with them

when I was a child. It did not matter that so much of
the roof was gone or that large parts of it were in dis-
repair. It held such a feeling of peace and wholeness
each week that I could not wait to visit on Sundays.
The Reverend was always kind and his stories filled
me with hope.'

'Why do you not still attend?'

'Fear.'

'Fear of what?'

'Much like you, I fear the unknown. What the men
said was partly true. While I am not a witch, I am
scarred from a boat accident with my father. I am a
recluse. I am awkward and unsure of how they will
react to both of those things. Will I be shunned? Will
I be laughed at or jeered at? And worse still, will I
not have that feeling of peace and wholeness that I
used to? Will it destroy the memory that I have of it
and of my parents in the meantime?'

'You cannot lose them or all of your memories
of them.' He paused and smiled. 'Unless, of course,
you end up attacked, almost drowned, and left to die
at sea because someone wants you dead for secrets
you cannot even remember. But that lot is not yours,
it is mine.'

She smiled and laughed despite the seriousness
of their talk. He was trying to put her at ease and it
was working whether she wanted it to or not. He slid
his hand closer to her own until the tip of one of his
fingers touched hers. The warmth and comfort of it
made her feel anchored, safe and…content.

It was an unfamiliar feeling.

Nay. That wasn't true. It wasn't unfamiliar, but it was a feeling she had not had in a very, very long time.

'And whatever scarring you have…' he said, his words as hesitant and uncertain as she felt. 'You should not hide it. It is a mark of what you have survived, like my own scars and bands of ink along my arms. It is a reminder of your will. Your strength.'

'Perhaps one day I will feel such contentment about it, but I am not so resolved to it as of yet.'

'We are quite the pair, you and I. You worry about forgetting the past and I fear I will never remember it. And as of late, I fear I may not like what I remember. What if I am a bad man, or a failure as a laird? What if there was good reason for them to try to kill me? What if the secrets that I know about the clan and about my father are so horrendous that I will not be able to live with myself once I discover what they are?'

The pain in his eyes and the dancing of the candlelight across his features made him seem younger. She could imagine him as a boy, then a young lad and finally the grown man he was now, struggling with goodness and wanting to always do the right thing. She understood. She had lived a very similar life. She had longed to do right even when justice was not possible.

She stared at his hand, wanting to hold it. Her heart fluttered at the thought. She slid her hand over his own and held it, savouring the comfort that such contact gave her. 'I cannot imagine you ever to be a cruel man or a failure at anything. You have had a miraculous recovery by your sheer will and desire to live. I gave you tinctures and clothes and food, but you chose to live. You fought to live. And I cannot believe that a man with such fight would ever allow any harm to come to those he loved or to his clan. Not intentionally anyway.'

He shifted his fingers so his thumb could caress the top of her hand, the unexpected intimacy of his touch making her breath catch. 'I can only hope, Iona MacKenzie, you are right and I can be the man you believe that I am.'

'I believe you already are,' she answered.

His thumb stilled. 'Your words bring me to my knees. I do not know where such faith in me has come from, but I am grateful for it, for hope, for you. It gives me strength.' His hold on her hand tightened. 'I worry I can never repay it.'

'I do not expect repayment.'

'I know you do not, but I want to help you. Do more than merely grind your tinctures or clean your dishes. What can I do?'

Kiss me.

She pressed her lips together, thankful the words only popped into her mind and did not escape her lips as she feared they might. 'What is it you wish to do?'

'What of your cottage? Can I help you in crafting a plan to ensure that it does not become seized by Chisholm for lack of payment? Perhaps we could devise a list of ways for you to increase your income or reduce your expenses, so you can repay him sooner

and not be at risk. I know you have said how important this cottage is to you and I would hate to be the
cause of you losing it. I know that I have cost you
time, food and resources by caring for me.'

What could she say to such a kindness?

He slid closer to the table, leaned forward and
gripped her hand. 'Please. Please allow me to help
you. Not only would it relieve some of my guilt at the
risk you are taking for me, but it will also distract me
from thinking too much about who those men were
and why it is they want so desperately to kill me.'

He smiled at that last part and she could not help
but smile back. 'You have a rather morbid sense of
humour, but I do understand. Work and distraction
have saved me many a time in my life.'

'So, it is agreed? We shall formulate a plan together
to help you protect this cottage?'

'Aye. But on one condition from me.' She leaned
closer to him as well, prepared to add in her own condition and knowing full well he would baulk at her
suggestion. 'You will allow me to help *you* discern
who is after you and why. We will be a team, you and
I. What say you?'

He shook his head and let go of her hand. 'I say
it is a horrible idea. These men could kill you just to
get to me. I could not live with myself if anything…'
He paused to rake a hand through his hair. 'You did
not hear them, Iona. They will let nothing stand in
their way to get to me.'

'I suppose I should be careful then, shouldn't I?'

He dropped his head into his hands and groaned. 'I should have known when I offered that this is what would have happened,' he said. 'I feel I walked right into a trap.'

'Not a trap, per se, but perhaps a well-laid snare.'

'Whatever you name it, you did so with a skill I am quite unnerved by,' he said with a chuckle. 'But, in all seriousness,' he added, his smile falling away, 'you must agree to be safe and not do anything to put yourself at risk. I mean it.'

'I understand. I would never do such. I have far too many furry mouths depending on me.'

'And me,' he added. 'I depend on you.' His words were a quiver hitting their mark, her stomach fluttering with his openness and vulnerability. He needed her.

And I need you.

But she was not brave enough to say it. Not yet anyway.

'I know that,' she answered. 'And I promise to be careful.'

He stood and moved back his chair, then extended his hand. 'No better time than the present.'

'Sorry?' she asked, staring up at him blankly. 'I do not understand.'

He wriggled his fingers out at her. 'The best way to be careful is to be prepared for anything.'

She frowned. 'And?'

'And I shall add to my list of chores a daily lesson in protecting yourself.'

'You think I cannot fend for myself?' she challenged.

'Nay. I think you believe you can protect yourself.'

She rolled her eyes at him and stood. 'Because I am a woman?'

'Aye.' He took a few steps to the centre of the room. 'And today shall be your first lesson.'

'And if I do not wish to have such a lesson?'

He lifted his brow. 'Then I will believe it is because you know I can best you, even blinded as I am.'

She stood and pushed back her chair.

He smiled. 'I knew that would get you,' he teased.

'You do know what rankles me, but I do not know if I would boast that as a skill to be proud of.'

'And why shouldn't I? It is just a well-placed snare, is it not?'

'You have made your point,' she replied. 'I am up and listening.' She popped a hand to her hips.

He lunged for her, and she barely moved out of the way in time.

He regained his footing and smiled. 'Nice reflexes. That shall be your greatest asset in protecting yourself. Other than your gut, of course. Instinct cannot be taught, so you must always listen to it.'

'I do. It has saved me more than once.'

He lunged at her again and he almost caught her sleeve.

'Do not be distracted by our conversation. A strike can happen at any time.'

She widened her stance and watched his movements as he shifted his weight from side to side on his feet, trying to discern which way he would move next. So far, she could see no pattern to his lunges. He stilled and so did she.

Then, he leapt at her, clutching her by the arm and tugging her to him, her back flesh to his chest. 'Do not let my lack of movement make you think I have given up the chase,' he said, whispering in her ear. 'That is when you should be most watchful. Your attacker will wait until you are feeling most comfortable to strike.'

Her breath was caught in her throat, her body painfully alert and taut to his touch and closeness. The sheer heat of him made her blood pulse and her core ache. If she wasn't careful, she would show him how weak he made her and give in to her desire to kiss him.

She elbowed him in the gut and freed herself instead. 'Perhaps,' she said with a smile, 'you should take some of your own advice, my laird, and not get too comfortable.'

He coughed, clutching his abdomen, then nodded. 'Perhaps,' he said and laughed. 'You are right.'

She let out a loud, fake yawn. 'I must retire, so I can get up early to put the nets out. I am exhausted from the day.'

And from fending off my feelings for you.

If she did not create some distance between them, she might give in to her body's desire to know what his lips would feel like on her own or roaming freely, nipping along the nape of her neck. She shivered at the imaginings and her body tightened painfully.

'Aye,' he answered. 'Till tomorrow, Iona.'

'Till tomorrow,' she replied, clutching her arms to her chest, willing her pulse to slow as she gathered up her blankets and readied for sleep.

Chapter Twelve

Royce woke to find Iona already gone. Funny how he could know she wasn't there without even being able to see. He was becoming highly attuned to her sounds, her smell and the way she made the air move when she was about. Twice he had almost kissed her yesterday. Despite his mind's knowing full well such an action was foolish, reckless even, his body ached for her, craving her heat and closeness. He'd wanted to feel every inch of her yesterday and foolishly did everything he could to create such intimacy of touch, words and feeling.

Had he always been so foolish with women? Or was Iona something special? His gut told him she was the latter. His attraction to her was more than physical, despite how he longed to claim her as his own. He wanted to share his secrets and fears with her, and he longed to hear her own.

In truth, he was beginning to care more about her than discovering who he was or the secrets and men that threatened his life, which was ridiculous. He could not stay on this island with her. They had no future. He was a laird and she a healer. He had a life elsewhere as much as she had a life here that she would never leave.

He rose and left the cottage, taking heed to listen for any noise outside and sending Jack out first. Once he felt it was safe to do so, he completed his ablutions with relative ease, having mapped out the number of steps to the outhouse as well as the manoeuvrings within once he was inside. He stood for a moment, soaking in the fresh air, and enjoying the sun on his face. Movement from behind startled him and he turned, ready to defend himself.

''Tis a good thing I am no stranger,' Iona said as she approached. 'Otherwise, we would all be found out and the ruse up. Why did you not wait until my return?'

His shoulders slumped. 'Boredom mostly.'

She thrust a smelly netting's worth of something from the sea into his hands, holding them with her own. 'You won't be bored now. You can set it outside for now until we can clean them,' she chided. 'But please, next time wait until my return. Something horrid could have happened and I find I am growing used to your company.'

Concern trumped her frustration at his foolhardy choice and he revelled in knowing she cared for him. Perhaps she had feelings for him as he did her. She slowly released her hands from his and walked past him into the cottage. He dropped the catch outside, followed her within and closed the door once he heard Jack scamper in behind them.

'Successful catch?' he asked.

'Somewhat, but there is enough fish to be eaten for tonight and some left to be dried for later this week.' There was something about the hitch in her voice that made him weary.

'And?'

She sighed. 'And they found a man dead along the shoreline. A stranger and quite a horrid death from what I overheard from two men heading out by boat. They say he was almost unrecognisable, but that his tattooing on his arm made them realise he was not from here. The bands they describe sounded like...'

'Mine,' he added, completing her thoughts. Royce swallowed hard. The implication was quite clear. He had not come alone and the man who had accompanied him was now dead, as Royce would have been if not for Iona. He sat down in the chair with a thud.

She joined him at the table. 'That was my first thought as well, but we might both be wrong.'

He frowned. 'Do you really believe that? Exactly how many strangers do you have coming to this isle?'

She conceded. 'Few. I just did not wish to believe it to be true.'

'Why was he not found until now? If he perished the night I was wounded, he should have been found soon after I was.'

'They said he was caught in some debris when the storm blew in. It was only in clearing it that the fishermen discovered him.'

'Poor man.'

'If he was indeed here to protect you,' she added.

'You think we could have fought and I killed him?' he asked. He shook his head in disbelief. 'I cannot fathom killing one of my own men, especially a brother in arms, if we shared the same ink bands. Nay. I won't accept that as a possibility.'

'Whether you accept it or not, there will be more searches along the island. More scrutiny. We will have to be even more careful.'

'You think they will search your home?'

'They will be certain to come this way. If you are discovered, you may be blamed for his death and me punished for aiding you in your recovery.'

'We cannot have that. We will launch an enquiry of our own to help save us both.'

'Oh? And how shall we do that?' she asked.

'You will tell me everything and we will devise a plan to discover more. And I will teach you more of how to protect yourself. Perhaps we shall even bury some well-placed traps about the cottage to know when and if people come by.'

'To alert us to them sooner?'

'Aye.'

'Sounds like a busy day. I suppose we should get started with the fish. Come. We will work in the barn. I cannot abide to gut the fish inside the cottage.'

Soon, the fish for the night were gutted and prepared and any extra salted and hung to dry, and traps of hidden ropes and holes were set along the outskirts of the cottage to help alert them to strangers. They retired to the cottage and set about working on the three new tinctures requested, so they could be delivered that eve.

Royce's mind spun with ideas on what exactly had brought him here and strategies to keep them safe, but he could not shake the feeling that Iona was keeping something else from him.

'Has something else happened? You have been quiet since your return this morn,' Royce asked as he continued the rhythmic grinding of the herbs with the pestle against the smooth stone mortar.

'Chisholm caught me as I returned from the beach. Asked me where his money was.'

'Ah. I remember. You told him you would bring it by. Have you not already done so?'

'Nay. I still do not have it all.'

'Then, merely give him what you have as a gesture of good faith.'

'I did, but it was not enough. He says he will turn me out in two weeks' time, if I cannot repay all I owe in full. And I will never have enough,' she said, a tremble in her voice. 'And to lose this place,' she said with a small sob, 'will be losing them.'

Royce ceased his work and rose, walking to the sound of her weeping. Without hesitation, he pulled her into his arms and gripped her tightly, hugging her to his body. She clutched him, sobbing into his neck, trembling against him as if she were the one lost on the shore this time needing healing and rescue.

'Iona,' he murmured, kissing the top of her head, 'we will do everything we can to keep that from happening. And either way, you will not lose them. They are in your heart, your mind, and are part of who you are.'

She pushed at his chest to create distance between them. He reluctantly released his hold. 'That is easy for you to say,' she hiccupped. 'You have a family elsewhere. I have no one.'

He stilled, his chest tightening. 'Easy for me to say?' He let go of her. His breaths were ragged, and he fisted his hands by his side. 'You *choose* to have no one. You could walk into town tomorrow and take part in a life, but you do not wish to. You have a choice. I have no choices. I have but a handful of disordered memories. I do not even know if the people I remember are alive. I have no home. I have nothing…but you.'

Chapter Thirteen

Iona stared at Royce, revelling in his fierce beauty. His chest heaved and his eyes were wild. The sheer desperation and anger in his voice should have served as a warning to her. *This* was the raw and unyielding ferocity she had felt in him that first day, even as he lay unconscious in her cottage. The desperation to live that had brought him clawing up the shores with his last bit of strength, the stubborn will that had kept him alive and now his vicious challenge to her words when she had begun to feel sorry for herself.

She should hate him for what he had said, but she could not...for it was true, whether she wished to acknowledge it or not. She *had* chosen this life. Chosen to be alone. But his situation was not the same. He had not chosen any of this. He was here with her now, tethered to her without his own choice to do so, and now as the danger around him mounted, he still told her the truth and challenged her. He would not allow her to wallow and, for some odd reason, she cherished it as much as it terrified her.

As much as *he* terrified her…well, not him so much as how she *felt* about him.

'What if I choose you?' she asked. The fire crackled in the background and rays from the sunset outside reflected off his features.

'Iona, I don't understand…' he said.

Before she changed her mind, she rushed to him, grabbed his face with her hands and kissed him. Not the chaste kiss of a woman unsure, but the heady eager kiss of a woman who needed the man she kissed. She felt the surprise ripple through the taut muscles in his upper body, which softened before gripping her fiercely, urgently.

One arm wrapped around her lower back and pulled her to him until she was flush against his torso, her leg resting between his own. The other hand wove through her hair and then kneaded the back of her neck as he responded to her kiss with a searing need she hadn't expected.

Acting on her emotions felt primal and wild and once she began she found it difficult to stop. His lips and hands were setting a trail of small fires where they went. When he touched her cheek, the unscarred one, fear jolted her back and she pulled away. She panted for breath, realising he had almost discovered her scar and she'd almost ruined the moment between them.

He stood waiting, uncertain, his breathing as ragged as her own. Desire burned in his eyes, which sent tendrils of want and longing through her. Her body vibrated with an unmet need that matched his own.

'You know how to bring a man to his knees, Iona MacKenzie,' he said, his voice husky and deep. 'If you hadn't stopped, I surely would have claimed you.' He ran a hand down his face.

She bit her lip at his admission. He wanted her as she did him. She took a step towards him and then stopped. What was she doing? She was about to set a fire she could not squelch. 'And if I'd let you, what then?' she asked, taking another step towards him.

He stilled as if struck dumb by her words. Then he took a step in her direction, one, then another, like a wolf hunting its prey. When he reached her and stood but a hand's length from her face, the toes of their boots almost touching, he pulled back his shoulders and lifted his chin. 'I guess we'll never know. Only a fool plays with such fire and I for one hope you are no fool.' His Adam's apple bobbed in his throat as he swallowed.

'I am no fool,' she whispered. 'I just wished to know...'

'Know what?' he asked, his voice tight and strained.

What it would be like to kiss you, so I can remember it when you leave.

'I must go,' she answered. 'There are deliveries to be made.'

Before he could ask more, she packaged up the completed tinctures, grabbed her basket and left.

An hour later, she climbed the hillside, crossing the last roll of beach before she reached her cottage. Off in the shadow of an abandoned fisherman's hut her gaze caught a flicker of movement and she stilled. Then she saw Jack jog out from behind the hut and almost cursed aloud. She scanned the area around her, lifted her skirts and hustled over to the hut.

'What are you doing out here?' she hissed, swatting Royce on the shoulder.

'Ow!' he replied, batting her hand away. 'Trying to gather information *and* make sure you returned safely. You seemed upset when you left.'

'And was Jack supposed to protect you?'

He didn't answer.

'Just as I thought. Hurry along. We must go back inside.'

He clutched her wrist. 'Nay. I don't wish to.'

'You sound like a petulant child,' she replied and he released her wrist. 'Come inside before you are discovered.'

'I cannot keep hiding in there when you leave, Iona. It will get me no closer to the truth. You and I both know that. I need to try to figure out why I came here. I can't do that hidden away.'

'Your memories will—'

'My memories are few and sporadic. If I merely wait until my memory returns, I may never find out the truth. And I need to know. Of all people, I thought you would understand this.'

She bristled. 'Why do you say that?'

He reached for her arm and gently held it. 'Because I know it plagues you not to know what exactly befell your father after the boating accident.'

She had no challenge. He was right. She was desperate to know the truth, but most likely would never know what happened after the accident that killed him and disfigured her and who had scavenged from his body along the shore.

'It is night. What do you hope to discover now?'

'I don't wish to spy, but swim. Swim with you. Teach me to swim again.'

She baulked. 'What? Why? How does that have anything to do with the past?'

'Because I keep dreaming of her, my sister Violet being pulled out to sea. It frightens me, terrifies me, and then I remember being attacked and almost drowning. If I cannot overcome my fear of the water, I will be paralysed further in my efforts to figure out what has happened to me. I will not tell you how long it took me to get this close to the loch. Even the sound of it unnerves me if I listen too long.

'But you, you love the water despite what happened to your father. I want to know how to do that. How to overcome my fear of the water, so I can move forward. I don't want to be trapped, whether it be in that bloody cottage or by the fears of my mind. Will you…' he said, 'will you help me?'

She didn't know what to say. He was asking for her help, gripping her arm and staring out into the dark abyss of night. He was brave, far braver than she. Perhaps she could learn from that bravery and attack some of her own fears and demons that kept her up at night.

'You are much larger than me and you cannot see,' she answered. 'Truth be told, it is dangerous. I don't know if it's safe, but I want to help you. I want to help you overcome your fear of the water.'

'What if I only wade into the shallow waters? That would be safe, wouldn't it?'

'Aye. It would be safer, but I worry about us being seen.'

'What if we waited until later in the eve? Midnight or so? Surely no one would see us then.'

His eagerness was contagious and she felt herself giving in slowly.

'As long as you agree to listen and do exactly what I say, then we will come back out later this eve and I will teach you to swim.'

'I will do exactly as you say. Thank you,' he replied, pressing a kiss to her cheek. He felt for the basket and took it from her gently. She slid her arm through his own to help guide him, or at least that was what she told herself. It couldn't be that she was growing attached to the feel of his touch or the warmth of his body next to hers.

Nay. It was nothing of the sort. Otherwise, she might have to admit that she was falling slowly in love with a laird who was destined to leave her feeling more alone than she already was. That she was an accomplice to her own heartbreak.

She pressed closer to him and the subtle friction of his body next to hers began a slow, steady hum along her limbs. She smiled. Nay. It was nothing of the kind.

They worked quietly in the hours before midnight. She worked on the new tincture orders as he ground up the herbs in the mortar and pestle and set about whitling her some new tools from the driftwood she'd found, which she discovered he was quite skilled at despite being blind. It was one of the many items she planned to sell in hopes of collecting more coin for Chisholm.

When the hands of the small mantel clock closed in and stacked neatly in place, one on top of the other upon the twelve, Iona set aside her work and wiped her hands on her apron. ''Tis time,' she said.

Royce rose from the table and set aside his blade and whittled driftwood. Soon, it would be a fine spurtle, fit for many uses.

'Best leave your boots and coat here,' she replied. She paused. What would he swim in? 'And your tunic. You can swim in your trews.'

Although he could have swum naked as she'd seen his form before, the idea of it made her throat dry.

'Aye,' Royce replied. He shucked off his boots, shrugged out of his coat and slung it around the chair back. Then he stood before he pulled his tunic over his head with one deft movement, exposing his finely sculpted torso. She fisted her hands by her side, fighting the urge to step forward and touch him.

He was a glorious-looking creature.

'Ready?' he asked, staring out towards her.

She stripped down to her shift quickly and set aside her clothes and boots. 'Aye. Now I am. Follow me. Come along, Jack.'

She set out, the slight breeze hitting her skin, and gooseflesh rose along her arms in anticipation of the water and of being with Royce. Saying no to his request would have been the wise and reasonable thing to do, but she was neither. There was a wildness raging within her. A craving for him that she didn't even understand, but one she could not deny. She wondered if he could also feel it, the tethering between them. No, not the tethering, but the pull that kept them bound to one another even in the quietest of moments.

She curled her toes into the sand and waited for him to reach her side. Soon, he settled in next to her and the back of his hand brushed hers. That slight touch felt like an ember catching fire under her skin and she sucked in a breath and commanded herself not to move. She would savour this for just a moment.

Closing her eyes, she heard the waves lapping in on the shore and the glorious silence of the midnight sky, while the softest of breezes brushed her hair along her face and neck. After taking a few more breaths, she opened her eyes and gazed upon Royce. He stared ahead into the sea, his muscles tight and his hands clenched by his sides. She lifted her hand and ran her fingertips along his shoulder and down his bicep, startled by the shivering she felt beneath. She stilled.

'Are you cold?' she asked.

'Nay. I am terrified,' he said quietly.

Her hand skimmed down his forearm and she laced her fingers through his own. 'Do not be afraid,' she replied. 'I will not let anything happen to you. All you must do is listen and follow my instructions. The water will do the rest.' She squeezed his hand. 'Ready?' she asked.

'Nay,' he replied, gripping her hand as if she were his lifeline. 'But we go forth anyway.'

'Let us take five steps together. Small steps for you and large ones for me. Then you will feel the water on your toes and we'll stand in that water until you're ready to take the next step. Agreed?'

He released a shaky breath and nodded. 'Agreed.'

And so she began the count. 'One…two…three…four and five.'

The cool water lapped up and back between her toes, under the soles of her feet and finally around the back of her ankles. She glanced over to see him taking in deep breaths, his chest rising and falling with irregularity.

'Deep breath in,' she said. 'And now a deep breath out.'

She walked him through his breathing until it levelled out and became more regular. 'You are doing well, Royce,' she said. 'Ready to take one more step or maybe even two?'

He nodded and gripped her hand even harder.

'One and two,' she said as they took two more steps and allowed the water to come up to their ankles.

He expelled a breath. 'I am not sure why I thought this was a good idea,' he said, his voice tight. 'My heart rages in my chest as if I were about to go into battle.' He chuckled and cleared his throat.

'You are. You are in a battle of memory. Your body and mind remember this as a threat. We must replace a new memory over the old, so your body and mind can see the water as something other than a danger.'

After another minute, she asked, 'Two more steps

and the water will be up to your thighs and we can practise floating and even some swimming.'

'Two more steps,' he murmured.

'Hold on tight,' she commanded. 'Do not let go of my hand.'

He chuckled. 'There is no danger of that.'

She stepped forward and he came along with her. The water ebbed and flowed around her waist even though the water only came up to his thighs due to their height difference. 'Take my other hand,' she said, reaching out so her other hand skimmed his fingertips. He seized her hand in his own and released a breath.

'Now lean back into the water while holding my hands. Slowly. Slowly. There you are,' she murmured, guiding him as he leaned back into the water. 'If you lift your feet and relax, you will float.'

'Are you sure?'

'Aye,' she replied. 'Trust me. And when you float, it is one of the most peaceful feelings in the world. As if you are cradled and held by some force greater than your own. As if you are held by life itself.'

'I will be happy to just survive.'

'Lean back and relax. There you are.'

He was floating, but he was anything but relaxed. Worry lines wove through his forehead and brow and his mouth was pressed into a thin line of concentration.

'Relax,' she whispered. 'I am here. Trust me to care for you. Trust the water to care for you.'

Minutes later, the worry lines had fallen away and his lips had parted. She couldn't help but smile at the peaceful picture he made. This large, ferocious man floating on the loch as the stars shone overhead. The water was working its magic on him as it always did for her. His hold loosened and she let one of his hands drift into the water and float out, while she held on to the other carefully.

He gripped her hand and started, kicking his legs in the water.

'I've got you,' she said, holding his hand and placing another on his shoulder. 'I think you almost fell asleep.'

'I think I did,' he sputtered, clasping her hand and pulling himself up to standing, 'but I felt like I was falling, being pulled under, and it startled me awake.'

'Is that what happened to your sister? Was she pulled away from you?'

'Aye. In my memory, she is caught in a current she could not escape from and I could not reach her before she was pulled out to sea.'

'You must swim against the undertow if that ever happens to you. Cut against it, so you can pass it but not be drawn into it and out to sea.'

'I suppose that makes sense. Just as one must cut across the battlefield rather than charging in head on. I can remember that,' he said. He ran a hand through his wet hair, the water sluicing down his torso and in and out of the crevices of his muscles.

It made her wish she were water. Her throat dried.

She pressed her lips together. 'Shall we return?' She needed to create some distance between them.

'Aye. I am cold and I imagine you are, too. I can

feel you trembling.' His thumb caressed the hand he still clutched for safety.

If only he knew how much jeopardy she was in now. How dangerous *his* proximity was.

While the cold was not the reason for her trembling, she would not admit to the truth. 'Aye. This is later than I usually swim.' She leaned back and wet her hair to distract herself from his beauty.

'Thank you for helping me get over my fear of the water,' he said, stepping towards her, the water lapping higher against her torso.

'Thank you for trusting me to help you.'

'I know I cannot remember,' he said. 'But I am quite certain I have never met a woman such as you, Iona MacKenzie. I wish I could tell you, show you...'

Chapter Fourteen

Royce meant it. He had never met anyone like Iona MacKenzie and he knew he never would again. It wasn't his memory telling him such, but his heart, his gut. He wanted to scoff at his own daftness for believing in such things, but he couldn't explain it otherwise.

He was drawn to her, a woman he hardly knew and couldn't even see, as if she were the missing part of himself he had searched for since the day he was born. He wanted desperately for her to know how much he cared for her. But the words that came to his mind were simple and useless.

He wanted to make love to her right now in the middle of the loch, in the water he had so feared but hours ago, to show her how he felt.

He wanted to claim her as his and never let her go. He needed to feel what he could not see and show her what he could never say in words.

But did she feel the same? Want the same?

He'd never know if he stood here staring into the darkness like a dolt.

He let go of her hand and let his own drift in the water as he walked closer. His hands slid along the cool tide until they found her and slid lightly along her sides, the thin, wet shift the only thing separating his fingertips from her skin. She sucked in a breath and her body tightened briefly before it relaxed.

He grasped her waist, tugging her closer, and she gasped in surprise, but didn't resist. He bent his head, nuzzling her throat, his lips skimming along her wet warm skin, so supple and sweet. She clutched the back of his neck as he continued a trail of kisses down her collarbone and licked the small lusty hollow of her neck.

All he could hear were her ragged breaths against his cheek and the subtle movement of water along the shore. She moved her hips against him and he shifted, cupping one of her buttocks with his palm.

'Royce,' she murmured, wrapping one and then the other of her legs around his waist and kissing him full on the mouth. The heady feeling of her core wound around him as she kissed him with such abandon made him lightheaded. He held her and stumbled back in the water. She tugged her lips away from his own.

'Inside,' she murmured and then kissed along his jawline. 'I will guide you.'

'You trust your well-being to a blind man?' he asked, trying to lighten the moment, as unsure of her request as he was of his ability to guide them back to the cottage unharmed.

'Nay,' she said, running her fingers along his cheek. 'I trust my well-being to you. You are far more than a blind man, Royce. Remember what you have learned. I believe in you.'

He hesitated.

'Take three strides and you will reach the shore,' she said.

'You are sure?'

'Aye. I am. You can do it.'

He took one step and then another, testing his footing before he continued. After a final step, he felt the cool air hitting his body and he knew they were ashore.

'Well done,' she said. 'You see, I knew you could—'

He seized her lips and she kissed him back, matching his urgency with her own, and his blood heated, his pulse raced, and all he wanted was to strip off his soaked trews and lay flesh to flesh with her on the sandy beach. He reached up to touch her face and she pushed him away.

'Royce,' she panted. 'Stop. I must tell you something,' she said.

He froze.

Bollocks.

Perhaps he'd misread what she wanted. Confused, he set her down on the ground and she held his arm. 'I'm sorry, Iona. I didn't mean to—'

'Nay. You did nothing wrong. I just…' she continued, then faltered once more.

He waited and she let go of his arm. The loss of her touch was immediate and consuming. He wanted to reach out to her, but knew he needed to wait for whatever it was she had to say.

'Come inside,' she whispered. 'There is something I must tell you, but not here.'

He followed her, but his steps faltered. The confidence he'd once had seemed to melt away or perhaps that was merely the dread of what he did not know or understand.

Had he misinterpreted her intentions so badly? Been so consumed by his own feelings that he had not recognised her own?

He stumbled into the cottage behind her. She dropped the latch and moved about the room, the anxiety evident in her uneven footfalls and louder than normal movements.

A fire began to crackle to life in the hearth and he stilled as he heard the movements of fabric on skin—in this case, her soaked shift being removed. He swallowed hard, but stood frozen, the water from his soaked trews and hair dripping on the floor.

'If you'll hand me your trews,' she offered, 'I can hang them by the fire to dry while we sleep.'

Rather than asking her what had happened, he stripped down and took the towel he offered her to dry his hair and body. Then he wrapped himself in the blanket she handed him as she took the wet towel away.

'Those men were right about me,' she said.

'About what?' he answered, following the sound of her voice by the fire. He slid down next to her, pressing his knee against her own.

'About what they said.'

'That you are a witch,' he teased.

She knocked her shoulder into him. 'Nay. I am still no witch. I am scarred.'

'I know that. Do you not remember? You told me of it already. It does not bother me.'

'But it bothers *me*. I am scarred on my face. Badly. It is one of the reasons I do not go into town and live such a life. I cannot bear the staring and the whispers. With you,' she continued, a tremor of emotion rattling her voice, 'I am not scarred and I am not scared.'

He stilled as her words fell to a whisper and his chest tightened. He reached out his hand, but stopped, not knowing if she wished for his touch or not.

'You may not remember,' she said wistfully, 'but the night I found you, you cupped my scarred cheek and told me I was beautiful. No one had said that to me in a very long time. I cherished it.'

'You *are* beautiful,' Royce said, his throat tight with emotion. 'You need hide nothing from me.'

She sniffed. 'You do not know if I am beautiful or not. You cannot see me.'

Royce shifted closer to her, letting the blanket fall from his shoulders, gazing at her without seeing. 'But that is where you are wrong. I do see you. I see every part of who you are, in here,' he said, pointing to his heart. 'You. Are. Beautiful.'

She couldn't breathe, her chest pushing and pulling with fear and longing battling within her. Her eyes welled.

He reached up his open palms to her. 'Please, Iona. Don't push me away.'

She waited to see if he would leave or abandon her in frustration. He did neither. He sat in silence and let his hands rest on his knees. He was waiting for her, not rushing her.

She bit her lip and risked everything.

She slid her palms against his own and then guided his hands to her. A tear fell down her cheek as his hands touched her face. There was no going back now. He would feel the horror of what she was and know the truth. He would finally know her, not the fairy-tale version she wanted him to see.

'How did this happen?' he asked as the pads of his fingers trailed tentatively along the raised edges and puckered skin.

'It was the boating accident that claimed my father during a bad storm. My face was cut badly when I was dashed against the rocks. I was lucky to have survived. As you know my father did not. He washed up to the shore days later, picked clean by the scavengers, both man and beast alike.'

'Does it pain you?' he asked, his brow furrowing as his fingers continued to move along the damage.

'Nay. Not anymore.'

He leaned forward and kissed her wounded cheek. Tears streamed down her face, and he wiped them away lightly. 'It does not bother you?' she asked, desperate to know if he still cared for her at all.

He smiled. 'Nay. If anything, I am more besotted by your beauty, if such a thing is possible.'

She tilted towards him, her blanket slipping down her back. Winding a hand around his neck, she rose slowly on her knees and kissed him so lightly she wasn't sure if their lips touched at all. The air between them was thick and charged, every part of her body humming. 'Kiss me.'

He hesitated and then kissed her slowly, so slowly that her body ached for more. She pressed her bare breasts to his chest and the shock of the sudden contrast of his heat and texture to her own stilled her for a moment.

'Lord above,' he murmured before he ran his hands along her bare back, tracing delicately along her spine, bringing her closer to him before kissing her once more. Her back arched in response, singing under his touch. She shifted, moving her legs over his torso, wrapping herself around his waist, revelling in the feel of him beneath her. She traced kisses along his jawline and he nipped along her neck, sending chills down to the tips of her toes.

'Iona,' he murmured, pausing in his endeavours along her throat. 'Are you sure this is what you want?' he asked.

'Aye,' she answered, guiding the blanket off him entirely. 'For the first time in a long time, I do not fear anything.'

'Not even coupling?' he asked. 'You are a virgin, are you not?'

'I am,' she answered suddenly nervous to say the words aloud, her fingers guiding his wet hair back behind his ear.

He cupped her cheek. 'I do not wish to take something from you that I cannot return.'

She stilled, gazing into his dark brown eyes. 'You cannot take something if it is given to you freely, can you?'

'Perhaps not,' he murmured, his brow furrowed. 'But I do not know if I am worthy of such a gift. What if I am pledged to another? What if I cannot fulfil the promise my body makes to you this eve?'

She stilled, uncertain by his words. 'And what promise is that? I do not expect a proposal, if that is what you worry of.'

He frowned, but leaned forward and rested his forehead against her own. 'But that is what you deserve, Iona. Do you not see that? I want to give you that, but I am not free to do so because I am trapped in some blank abyss of my mind. I do not even know who I am or what I can offer you, if anything at all.'

'You have given me more than I could have ever longed for. You have accepted me...for me.'

'As you have accepted me. Even when I was an arse when I woke, angry at the world, you kept me alive.' He smiled at her then. No almost smile, but a full smile of gratitude. 'Thank you.'

'Perhaps you can think of some other way of repaying me, my laird,' she asked, twining her hands around his neck.

His eyes flashed with mischief and he yanked the blanket off her. Her skin pebbled as the cool air hit her. 'Aye,' he answered, his voice husky and full of intention before lifting her in one deft movement, so that she was pressed intimately against him. 'I can think of a few.' He seized her mouth with his own as he carried her to the bed.

Chapter Fifteen

Royce woke in a delicious warmth that obscured the fact that he still woke to total darkness. Iona's smooth warm skin was draped along his body on one side while blankets covered the other. He shifted, letting his hand drift along Iona's back and long, unbound hair before resting along her head which lay tucked in his shoulder.

Her hair was smooth and smelled of the sea, while the rest of her held that same light floral scent that always seized his senses, sending them into high alert. Even now, his body was waking, thrumming to the tune of her flesh, wanting to ravish her once more.

He frowned. He was a cad.

He should hate himself for what he'd done and his lack of will power. Would the old him have given in to the request of a virgin such as herself and bed her with no promise of what he could and could not give her for her future? He might never know. His memory seemed locked away far out of reach, just like Iona. At least he'd taken precautions to prevent a child, by not spilling his seed within her, but even so, he'd acted poorly.

And even with those words streaming through his mind, his body desired her. He let his hand drift along her torso and on to her breast, which rested against his chest, his fingers teasing along the nipple there until it tightened. She stirred and he cursed himself. He pulled his hand away and covered his eyes.

Had he always been so selfish? He hoped not.

She ran her hand down his torso where it tentatively grazed his shaft that was already thickening and desiring her again.

'Iona,' he pleaded. 'Your touch is exquisite torture.'

'As is yours. Your touch woke me and set my body aflame. I am just repaying your kindness,' she teased.

Bloody hell.

She did it again with a bit more confidence this time and he thrust his head back in pleasure, unable to subdue his body's response or gain any control over the situation.

'And here I was trying to remind myself that I had already acted poorly and that I would not allow myself to join with you again,' he said through clenched teeth. 'Saints be,' he murmured as she leaned over him and left soft feathery kisses down his chest and then his abdomen.

Jack's bark from across the room startled them. Iona stilled and then clambered off him.

'What is it?' he asked, shaking his head to try to get his logic flowing once more and to clear the foggy webs of lust from his mind.

There was no answer. He rose from the bed, throwing off the blanket, and feeling for his trews which were scattered along the floor. He quickly pulled them on. 'Iona?' he whispered.

This was the part of blindness he could never get used to. The dependence on others and his inability to protect anyone. It went against everything he was. His deepest and most raw instinct was to control and prevent harm to those he loved.

Loved?

He stilled. He shook off the thought as he didn't have time to analyse it further. Jack barked once and then again. Royce could hear the creature's alarm as the pitch climbed higher and higher and his barks became more frequent and staccato. Whatever was happening wasn't good.

'There are men by the shoreline,' she whispered. 'And I have no idea why.'

'Tell me more,' he commanded, walking towards the sound of her voice as he reached her side. 'What time of day is it? What are they wearing? How are they standing? Does it look like they're planning a search? Or an attack?'

She rested a hand upon his shoulder. 'It is still dark, so they cannot see us. Do not worry. Jack was just doing his job in alerting us.'

If only he was as useful. He walked away from her and ran a hand through his hair, restless to know more and do more.

'There appear to be a group of six men in total,' she said. 'Chisholm is there, but some of these other men I do not recognise, but it has been a while since I have kept up with the newcomers in the village.'

Royce ceased his pacing. He swallowed his withering pride and tried to focus on solutions. 'What else do you see?'

'They have lanterns and a map. Perhaps they are planning a more detailed search or something else has happened. I could go out and ask.'

He cringed. 'I hate this,' he snapped. 'I should be the one taking care of you, not you always caring for me. What kind of man would let you go out in the dark of night and risk your safety?'

He was angry, so angry. He'd had enough of this blindness and lack of memory. He'd had enough of being hidden away and protected by a woman he should be protecting. He scrubbed a hand down his face and cursed.

'What has got into you?' she asked.

'I am enraged by my body and by my limitations. I am tired and fatigued of being so worthless to you. I am a child like this, not a man. I cannot care for you or protect you as I wish and as I should. How can you even stand to look upon me?'

'You are being a fool,' she replied. 'Your sight and your memory will be restored. Then you can hover and fret and protect me all you want. What you suffer now is temporary.'

'You think me a fool?' he said, incredulous at her words. 'I think it is you who is being a fool to think that I will regain my sight and my memory and be able to offer you anything. I may even have a family elsewhere and not even know it. Why would you ever wish to tether yourself to me?'

His chest was heaving and his breaths were ragged and irregular, as if he were being chased by a predator. Perhaps that predator was himself. He didn't know why, but he couldn't stop the anger and frustration spewing out of him. He knew he was destroying the beautiful fragility of what they had woven together these last few days in this cottage. It was as if he was outside his body, watching himself set fire to it all, but not being able to stop what would be a catastrophic end between them if he didn't.

'Why do you always do this?' Susanna said, her voice laced with accusation and fury.

'Do what?' Royce said flatly, running his blade over the whetstone in his other hand, largely uninterested in her words. He'd heard them a time or two before.

'Blow up everything that is good,' she replied, grabbing his wrist to cease his sharpening.

'What do you speak of, Sister? All I am doing is what is required of me as future laird of the clan.' He clicked his gaze up to her, annoyed by the interruption to what he always saw as a calming task.

'Severing your relationship with a woman who loves you is not duty, but foolishness.'

He shifted uncomfortably on the bench he sat on in the weapons room and rolled his eyes. 'Love is of no consequence to my duty as future laird. You may not know that, but I do. Father has all but drilled into my mind that my sole purpose is to care for and propel this clan to be the greatest in all the Highlands. She has little to offer to enrich our standing.'

His chest tightened at the thought of her. Alena was a kind, beautiful woman and he had never wished for her to become so attached to him. It had never been his intent to hurt her, but he had also never gone to great pains to explain his situation and what was required of him as first son.

'She? Will you not even use her name?' Susanna replied.

He gritted his teeth and stood. His anger was getting the better of him once more. 'I have had enough of your rebuke, Sister. You will leave and never speak of her again.'

'I would expect nothing less, Brother. It takes far too much energy for you to feel anything. It is as if when Violet disappeared, she took your heart with her.'

'Do not dare,' he growled, 'blame Violet for anything. You will never speak ill of our sister who is gone. Get out. Now.'

'Royce? Royce?'

He felt a gentle squeeze on his bicep and he blinked back to the present.

Iona.

'Did you just remember something?' she asked.

'I need a moment,' he murmured and felt for a chair, which she guided him to. He cupped his head in his hands and the memory played once more in his mind. Had he always been so cold? And who was this Alena woman? And why had he been so cruel to just cast her aside when her family could not add to his clan's favour and position in the Highlands?

Was he truly so cruel?

His hands shook. No doubt, he once was.

Was he still?

He had bedded Iona without any promise to her and had little if anything to offer her. So, perhaps not as cruel, but as selfish and as foolish. What would he do now?

He stood, desperate for air. 'I will return,' he said.

She clutched his hand. ''Tis too dangerous. They may hear you.'

'Perhaps that is what I hope for. To be found. To be punished. Who even knows what I may or may not have done?'

She cupped his face. 'I know you. You could not have killed anyone unless it was justified.'

'Iona, you cannot know me for I do not even know myself.' He pulled his hand away from her own and walked outside. He was desperate for air and space, and he was grateful she did not follow him out of doors or prevent him from leaving. The world felt as if it was closing in upon him and he could scarce breathe.

Once outside, the cool air hit his chest and face, and some clarity finally came to him. While he could not undo whatever was his past, he could adjust his future and that meant finding a way to help Iona and find out the truth about his own life. He could pledge nothing to her without knowing who he was. He closed his eyes, determined to do both if it was the last thing he did.

But where to begin?

Voices carried across the horizon. He stilled and focused in on their words.

'There is a chance we find nothing,' one man said.

'And there is also a chance we find everything. The man is alive. I feel it in my bones and, if he is found and discovers the truth, it will bring ruin upon us all. Keep looking,' the man ordered.

'I hope you know what yer about. Webster will be none too happy to know we've risked coming this close to the cottage. The woman is dangerous.'

'Webster won't know anything unless ye speak of it, ye fool.'

A smack sounded.

'What did ye do that for?' the man complained.

'Get back to work. The sun will be up soon and our opportunity will be gone with it.'

Webster.

There was that name again. It rang a bell in Royce's memory and he concentrated until the flash of his first memory flared back to life in his mind. Webster was the man Royce sought in his journey here. Who was he and what did he know? Perhaps Iona knew. He took his time and carefully returned to the cottage, mindful to close the door silently, so no echoes would be heard across the way where the men searched.

When he came in, Iona said nothing. Royce felt the tension in the air. She was right to be angry with him. Hell, he was angry with himself. He'd spouted off to her for no reason. She had been an easy mark for his frustration.

'I am sorry,' he said softly. The words were not so hard to say this time, as if his body was becoming more at ease with them as well.

She said nothing but slid her arms around his waist and hugged him tightly. They stood together without words for long minutes until she pulled back from him.

'Better?' she asked.

He smiled. 'Better.'

'They are searching quite intently.'

'Aye,' he whispered. 'They search for me still and believe I can cast ruin upon them all, but how? I also overhead talk about a man named Webster and how he was the one desperate to find me. But why?'

'Webster is not a man, but a woman,' Iona replied. 'She is called by her surname. Always has been.'

He froze. 'A woman?' he said. How could that be? His mind spun. That changed everything. He was even more confused and unsure.

'Tell me more about her,' he asked.

'Why are you so interested?'

'I finally remembered the name they mentioned in my first memory from when I was tossed overboard. It was Webster. I was supposed to be meeting a person named Webster, but I had assumed it was a man. Webster holds the key to why I came here. I must speak with her.'

'That may prove difficult. No one has seen her in over a decade. She is more reclusive than even me. I have heard some speculate about whether she is truly still alive or not.'

He baulked. 'Why would people pretend she was alive? What difference would it make?'

'A great difference. Her father owned a quarter of the island and made the male relative that was to inherit promise to allow Webster and her sons to stay on in the main house until Webster passed. If she is dead, then the house, its cottages and all its contents revert to her second cousin.'

'And who is her second cousin?'

She sighed. 'Chisholm. And he already owns a quarter of the island in his own right. If he inherits her quarter, then he will own half of the bloody island. And he will call in every loan he can to get enough monies to buy out the other half. He has always dreamed of uniting the island.'

'By owning all of it?'

'Aye,' she answered.

'That doesn't sound like unifying as much as controlling.'

'My point exactly. No one on the island is excited about such a future, so if she has passed many would feel compelled to hide such a fact.'

'Perhaps that is why the men came to meet me in her stead. And when I pushed on such matters, they knocked me out rather than reveal the truth.'

'Seems very plausible.'

'But why did I wish to see her in the first place? It is all such a puzzle.'

'If you think Webster has the answers, I will bring you to her home.'

'And then what would I do?'

'I am not exactly sure—maybe just ask?'
'Could it truly be so simple?' he asked in disbelief.
'It could be. Not everything has to be difficult.'
'Let us hope you are right.'

Chapter Sixteen

Iona tread carefully along the waterfront, her boots gripping the craggy rocks as a light wind made her cloak flutter against her body. While one of her hands felt along the large boulders and shrubs that lined the yard, acting as the wall separating the Webster property from the shore, her other hand clutched Royce's fiercely to guide him along an unknown terrain. They had done well so far in their silent travels with only occasional missteps. They could communicate without words or sight, and his trust in her was exquisite and unexpected, as if their bodies were finely tuned to the other's movements.

And maybe they were after the previous night of lovemaking.

She wondered if all people felt that way after such an intimacy. She wanted to ask Royce but didn't dare. He'd been quiet since their discovery of the men along the beach this morn, lost in thought. While he said it was his way of strategising and working through his new memories, she wasn't so sure.

Doubt niggled along her skin. She worried the silence was far more sinister and akin to regrets related to her. A pebble skidded out from beneath her walking boots and she set aside her worries. Focusing on the task at hand was essential.

Visiting the Webster property was far more difficult than she had led Royce to believe. If he'd known the risk, he would have denied the idea outright, so Iona had kept some of the finer details from him earlier in the morn when they'd first discussed it. The cloudy night sky had helped to mask their journey so far and she was grateful they had travelled such a distance without being seen or recognised.

The regular weekly gathering of the more influential men in the town at The Laughing Goat Inn worked in their favour as it meant fewer people would be out and about with a lower risk of discovery. Being mindful to keep to the less-frequented route along the shoreline also helped, despite its more precarious path. Royce tripped over a root, but Iona was quick to steady him as he collided into her side with a curse. He shifted away from her quickly and she frowned.

It was another reminder of how he'd been a bit physically detached and distant from her since they'd woken and been interrupted by Jack's barking earlier in the morn. There hadn't been any lingering touches from the night before or even a rogue kiss to her cheek. Just a polite reserved distance. One that made her skin chill.

She wanted to believe it was all due to his concern

over the men searching along the shore so early in the morn rather than him having second thoughts about making love to her the night before. The idea of him having regrets cut her to the quick, just as the idea of losing him gutted her. He had made her feel whole, beautiful and…as though she was enough.

A feeling she hadn't had since she was a wee girl when her parents were still alive. He had filled part of the empty chasm of loss that had plagued her for so long and she cherished it. She only hoped he did, too, but she didn't dare ask. Why risk getting an answer you don't want? Why risk caring for him more than she should at all?

The tiny baby goat pleaded for its mother, the pained cries setting Iona to tears.

'Father, why will she not let him eat? He is hungry,' she sniffed, running her hand down the baby goat's small frame.

He set his palm to her shoulder. 'He is the runt and she does not believe he will survive. So, she denies him milk to provide more to the others who, she believes, have a stronger chance to live.'

Iona wiped her eyes. 'But he can still live. Look at him. He is a beautiful creature. All he needs is some extra care.'

'Perhaps, but who shall give it?' he enquired. 'Your mother is busy with tinctures and I must gather the day's catch.'

'I will!' she'd offered, joy filling her every pore. 'Just tell me how, Father. Please.'

He'd smiled down at her then. 'You will care for him in addition to your other chores?'

'Aye, Father. I promise. I will even skip my swim so I can nurse him.'

'Then I will teach you, Little Fish, for your heart is as big as the ocean. Just remember to be patient. It will take time, perhaps even more time than you expect. He must learn to trust you and you must accept that his mistrust is not your fault and be patient, for his mother has rejected him. His heart is broken.'

'Iona?' Royce whispered, tugging her hand and yanking her from the past.

Her chest tightened as the memory faded away and she returned to the present. She blinked back the tears filling her eyes and swallowed down the emotion clogging her throat.

'Aye?' she answered, her voice raspy.

'How much further?'

''Tis not long. We come upon the edge of her property now. So far, it looks deserted. Not a single torch is lit inside and no smoke plumes from the chimney. I think they have all left for the inn. It makes me believe the stories are true and that Webster is long dead.'

Royce's shoulders slumped. 'As I feared. Now, how will I ever discover the truth?' He let go of her hand and rubbed the back of his neck, his eyes glittering in the moonlight.

'We will find a way,' she replied, thinking back on how many nights she had nursed that baby goat and what a fine young animal he had become, full of spunk and life. She smiled at her own foolishness and shook her head. Royce was no baby goat. He was a grown man, temporarily lost to be sure, but he would find his way with or without her. Her task now was to help him discover the answers he deserved.

He didn't answer, but lifted his hand to her shoulder, his cue to her that he was ready to continue, so she began the most dangerous portion of their journey, the passage through the back yard. It had been so long that she didn't know if they had any dogs any more.

Webster had loved her hounds and had had a pack of dogs every time Iona had passed this place when she was a girl. They had been a cheery collection of beasts from what she could remember, most of them outcasts from other families or too old to serve their hunting purposes. It was the one bit of softness she'd ever seen in the woman. Otherwise, she was prone to fussing at the children who passed her yard, forever accusing them of trampling her flowers.

She never liked guests on her property and hated that many a child cut through her yard to save looping around the bend to reach her small dock that was perfect for fishing. More than once Iona had seen her setting the dogs on any lads heading in that direction, reminding them that the dock was not a public one and that they were stealing her fish if they attempted to cast their nets or lines there.

Iona and Royce walked towards the back gate. She paused and scanned the yard. Upon seeing it empty, she lifted the latch and swung it open. The gate door screeched loudly, perhaps from lack of use, and Iona cringed.

Blast.

Royce increased the grip on her shoulder, his signal to hold fast and so she did, studying the dark surroundings. Despite the noise, there was no movement from within the house or the yard. Perhaps they were all alone. She released a breath and continued. They moved through the yard quickly to avoid detection, then ended up outside the back door. Iona bit her lip and softly tried the handle.

Locked.

Drat.

She scanned the surroundings and spied the root cellar. She smiled. From what she remembered, the root cellar was not any old root cellar, but connected to the bottom level of the house. But it was also small. Perhaps too small for a man like Royce to navigate, seeing or not seeing. First, she needed to discover if it was even open. They moved across to the root cellar door. Iona bent down and tugged. It squealed open and she rolled her eyes.

Evidently, it also wasn't frequented, which was odd. Why not use such a space if you had it? She certainly would have. It was pitch black and smelled of damp earth. Did she even want to try to go in? Glancing over to Royce, she knew he would have gone in for her.

'I'm going to try to get in through the root cellar,' she told him. 'Alone.'

'What?' he asked, grappling for her hand. 'You can't go in alone.'

'I can and I must,' she replied. 'It is too narrow a space for you.'

'It is too great a risk,' he said.

'We have already risked too much to turn back now,' she replied and squeezed his hand before letting go. She disappeared down the dark stone stairs and ignored his objection. Soon, her eyes adjusted to the darkness and she was able to make out faint lines of the cellar, which appeared largely empty.

'Iona?'

She froze. Had the man followed her in? She turned to see him gingerly testing his foot out to find each stair and his outstretched hand was before him to navigate any ceiling. If she wasn't so impressed by his sheer determination, she might have chided him. She walked back to the bottom of the stairs and guided him down by the elbow. He was stooped over to accommodate the low ceiling.

'What happened to waiting?' she asked.

'I will wait, but down here,' he answered. 'If something goes wrong, at least I will hear you and offer aid. Up there I am exposed and so are you.'

'You have a point.'

'What now?' he asked.

She scanned the cellar, trying to locate where she believed the stairs would be. Straight ahead seemed the most logical option, so she took one step after another and ended up at a wall. She felt along it, but only discovered shelves and dry herbs arranged upon them. Finally, she located another set of stairs.

'I'm going up. Please stay here.'

'Be careful,' he replied.

She took a careful step and climbed with her arms out ahead of her to determine where the door might be above her. After several steps, her palms came up on the door and she pushed it open. To her surprise, it opened as quietly as a whisper. She stepped out into the upstairs room and her eyes adjusted to the change in light. While it was still dark, it was not the pitch black of the cellar.

'What is it ye want?' a woman asked, her older age evident in the shake and tenor of her voice.

Iona froze and her pulse raced. It was Webster. She would recognise that gravelly voice anywhere; it mattered not that it had been over a decade since she'd last heard the woman's voice.

She cringed. How had she not seen the woman? Where was she? Behind her?

'I said, what do ye want?'

'Information,' Iona risked saying. If she were already discovered, what was to be lost by asking for the truth? She swallowed hard. Perhaps she should have thought this through. She might well be killed.

'Information? Ye broke into my home to talk?' she scoffed. 'Ye aren't much of a thief, are ye?'

'Nay. I am no thief. I just wish to speak to you.' Iona pressed her lips together and waited. She clutched her cloak and scanned the room, but still, she could not see the older woman.

'About?'

Iona paused. Now that she was here, she wasn't sure how to get the information she needed without mentioning Royce by name.

'Best spit it out, lass. Otherwise, leave. I've no time for uncertainty.'

Iona hedged. Was she endangering Royce by telling her of him? Or was it the only way he would find answers? Knowing Webster, the latter was the one way forward. 'About Royce.'

'Ah. Then ye'd best come in where I can see ye.'

Iona walked into the small room towards the sound of the woman's voice. As she approached, she began to see the profile of the petite woman who sat engulfed in a large chair covered with a blanket. The room was cold and damp without a candle lit or a fire burning in the hearth. It was altogether odd.

'Shall I light a candle?'

'Nay,' the woman answered.

Iona continued until she stood a few feet before the old woman who stared blankly out in the distance and Iona finally understood: the woman was blind.

'As ye now know, I cannot see ye, lass, but I am pleased ye came in so bravely anyway. Who are ye?'

'It is me, Iona MacKenzie, Mistress Elspeth.'

She spat on the ground. 'If ye know me at all, which I know ye do, girl, ye know I despise that name. Call me Webster.'

'Webster,' Iona said. 'I came to ask you about the information Royce sought upon his journey here. He was set to meet you. What did you have to share with him?'

'That depends. Where is he? Is he here? Perhaps slinking back in the shadows like the rest of them are prone to do.'

'The rest of them?' Iona asked, ignoring the old woman's venomous enquiry about Royce and taking a few steps closer.

'Aye. I regret ever becoming involved in my father's secrets. The only thing that ever came of them was harm and misery. It was his selfishness that killed my mother.' She rubbed her gnarled hands together, restless and on edge. 'And I shall never forgive him for it.'

'Could you tell me about those secrets or at least about the one involving Royce and his family?'

Webster laughed. 'How long do ye have, wee lass?'

'Until your sons return. I would prefer they not know of my visit.'

'And I would as well. They are a protective lot and prone to act first and question later, just like their father was.' She shifted uneasily in her chair and groaned.

'Can I do anything to ease your comfort?' Iona asked, unable to suppress her innate desire to care and nurture.

''Tis kind of ye to ask, child, but nay. Only tinctures help and I have had my fill of them today. Sit. I shall tell ye what I can without putting ye at further risk in exchange for tinctures, free of charge, mind ye, and delivered without my boys knowing.'

Iona faltered, but what choice did she have? 'How many?' she asked.

'Three a week. The healer my boys use does little good for me, but ye… I have a feeling ye have more of the gift.'

She bit her lip and then agreed. 'Three a week it is.'

'We have an agreement then. But do not say I didn't warn ye. Those that know the truth seem to not be long for this world.'

Saints be. The hairs on Iona's arms stood on end. She wanted to flee, but then thought of Royce. He deserved the truth no matter how horrid it was.

Iona swallowed hard and found a small wooden chair near the woman and sat on the edge of it, ready to flee in an instant if her sons returned early.

'It all started well before I was even born. This foul plan to support the Camerons in their quest to control the Highlands. My father's people were small but proud and they believed if they had an alliance with the Camerons, their worries would be over and they would be protected.'

'Were they not?'

She scoffed. 'We were protected, all right, but at what cost? The things they asked my father to do were…unspeakable. All in the name of fulfilling their end of their agreement to one another.' She shook her head.

'And Royce? Did he reach out to you, seeking the truth?'

'Aye. Fool of a man, he did. He didn't know what he was unearthing. Poor sot still doesn't. I sent my boys to warn him off, but it didn't work. Otherwise, ye wouldn't be here sniffing about. While I hadn't puzzled out what happened to him before, I do now. Ye saved him, didn't ye, my wee sea witch?' She snickered at her.

Iona said nothing, stunned by the woman's guess as to what she had done.

'A soft-hearted fool like yer parents. But that is a matter for another time.' She shook her head and Iona clenched the material of her gown, angry and bitter about the woman's callous attitude about her parents. The chair squeaked as she shifted upon it.

Sailor's fortune.

Iona rolled her eyes and sat on her hands to prevent the litany of frustration fall from her lips. If she didn't need this information so badly for Royce, she would tell the old crone just what she thought of her.

'She is no soft-hearted fool,' Royce replied, his words biting but soft.

When she turned to see his face, the hairs on her arms stood on end. She had never seen him look so severe, so angry. Her throat dried.

'Ahh...' Webster replied and smiled. What little light there was caught the gleam of the sporadic teeth that remained in her mouth. 'There he is, the Laird himself. I told the boys that ye would come if ye were indeed alive. That such searches of the island were a waste of time. Always allow the prey to come to ye, I reminded them. A might bit easier that way, but they never listen. They think I'm daft and senile. The loss is theirs, not mine any more. My days are numbered. I know that and so do they.'

'I am afraid I am out of pity for you, old woman. I need answers.'

'My, you are cut from the same cloth. You Camerons. All the same. Greedy and powerful and consumed by the need to keep it that way. So, what is it you seek?'

'I am a Cameron?' he asked.

She frowned. 'What joke is this? You are Royce Cameron, are you not? The same bastard that wrote me again and again begging for information on what yer fool of a father had written about in his bloody journal?'

Iona's eyes widened. She'd never heard a woman speak such to another man before, especially a laird. She glanced at Royce, who seemed equally shocked by her rudeness.

To her surprise, Royce's lip quirked into that almost smile she was so fond of. He came closer, resting his hands along her father's old waist belt and the small dagger that hung about his waist.

'Aye. I believe I am to be that same bastard you speak of.'

She scoffed. 'Ye are not sure? Are ye addled?'

'A bit,' he replied. 'I have few coherent memories after yer sons gave me a knock about and tossed me into the ocean. I am alive solely because of Iona. I owe my life to her, so take care as to how you dare speak of her.' That hard, stony look was back in his eyes.

'Hmm… Perhaps ye aren't cut from the same Cameron cloth. Sounds like ye may love the lass. That is a surprise. Perhaps yer sister is not the only one tainted.'

'Tainted? What does that mean?' Iona asked, no longer able to stand by and just watch the exchange, her interest piqued.

'Ye know exactly what it means, lass.' She coughed and wiped her mouth.

'Are you suggesting she is not a Cameron? Or that I am not a Cameron?' he challenged.

'I know one of ye wasn't. It was a secret yer father went to great pains to hide. Kept us with coin for decades to keep it quiet.'

'And now?' he asked.

'Now, I care little. I am dying and just wish it over. What my sons choose to do to you is their own making. Sounds like they decided to just do away with ye and the whole business. Can't blame them. Secrets eat away at ye, like they did with my husband. Didn't have the stomach for them.'

'Then, why did they attack him?' Iona challenged. 'If it is truly done with and of no concern.'

She shrugged. 'To protect me and make me proud. To keep ye quiet and bring an end to such misery. All that sniffing around made them nervous. We didn't know yer father had taken a liking to inking all of his secrets to paper. That was a nasty surprise. Who knows what all he mentioned?'

'Well, it wasn't enough for me to determine what he was referencing. Otherwise, I wouldn't have come here at all.'

'I suppose. Was still odd. A laird coming here in

secret with only one man for protection. Apologies for him, by the way. The boys got carried away.'

Iona's chest tightened. 'What happened to him?'

'Dead, I'm afraid.'

Chapter Seventeen

The woman wasn't well. Iona could see that now, but Royce couldn't. There was an unsettling gleam to her gaze that warned Iona to run and that whatever truth she told would come at too great a cost. Iona took another step back and grasped Royce's hand in her own and squeezed it. She prayed he would know what such a gesture meant.

Voices carried in from outside through the thin cottage walls.

'Nothing to say now?' she said. ''Tis almost time for you to meet my boys. They will be much pleased to see that you have stayed on to chat. It means they will not have to waste more time searching for ye and I will have my wish that ye are dead and the secret along with it.'

Iona tugged at Royce's hand. 'We must go,' she warned.

'Nay,' he growled. 'Not until she tells me the truth. We have not come so far for nothing. A man died to help me unearth it. I will scare it out of her if she wishes.'

Iona tugged at his hand. 'Do not get too close. Something ails her. She is not well,' she whispered.

The old woman laughed. 'Ahh. Not too bad, sea witch.' She took another swig from her tankard.

'Why did you ask for tinctures from me? Make me agree to bring them to you if you had already planned…this?' Iona asked.

'I wished to know if you would. You have the weakness of a healer's heart just like your parents.' She shook her head. 'Best ye set aside such fancies for your own well-being. Such kindness will be yer undoing, lass. Leave this Cameron be. He will bring ye nothing but pain.'

She took another swig.

'You will tell me what I need to know,' Royce demanded. His pulse throbbed through the hand Iona gripped fiercely to keep him a distance from the old woman. Who knew what she would do next?

'Or what? Ye will kill me? I am no longer interested in this world,' she said and coughed. 'But before I leave it, I will tell ye to cease yer enquiries. Nothing will come but despair if ye survive my boys and continue this course. Leave here. Burn that bloody journal. If ye don't, ye will only ruin what little goodness remains in yer clan and yer family. Let the past go.'

She coughed and shook. Whatever she drank was taking its affect now. While Iona wasn't sure, it looked to be hemlock. The sudden paralysis of the woman's system was horrifying to witness. Iona clutched Royce's hand and dragged him back to the root cellar door, guiding him down the stairs in front of her, taking care to guide the rug over the door in the floor as best she could as she closed it slowly. A moment later there was a thud and then an eerie silence. Iona and Royce stood nestled in against one another on the stone stairs, listening.

The front door opened and then slammed shut.

'Why is it so dark in here? The fire has gone out. Mother must have fallen asleep by the hearth again.' The man laughed, his words slightly slurred from perhaps a pint too many at the inn.

'Aye. I'll gather the flint and some tinder from outside,' the other man said.

Iona pressed a palm to Royce's back. 'Take three more steps down and we shall be at the bottom,' she whispered, her lips touching the shell of his ear.

He didn't move. She squeezed his hand. 'We must go,' she pleaded. 'It isn't safe to stay here.'

She could almost feel his internal struggle. His battle within. He cursed and then nodded before taking the first step down. They moved with trepidation, listening for any sign that the men had discovered their beloved mother's body. As Royce and Iona reached the floor of the cellar, a shout sounded above them.

'Mother?' a man called, followed by boots landing hard on the floor above them as he ran to her.

'Mother!' The other son came inside and rushed to the room above soon after.

The time Iona thought they had to escape before the woman's body was discovered was far less than she expected.

'Ten steps and we will be at the stairs going up

to the yard,' Iona stated. Her heart hammered in her chest as she resisted the urge to run. They had to be quiet to remain undetected and them falling in this pit of a cellar would only alert the men to their presence. They wouldn't be safe until they were back in her cottage, but a vast distance and many obstacles stood in their way. The first was this cellar, a dark maze. Why hadn't she paid better attention when they'd come in?

She frowned. Probably because she was so concerned by what other creatures might well be lurking down here. She shivered and Royce pulled her closer. This time, he turned to her and offered her reassurance. 'Stay close,' he said. 'I will get us out of here and safely home.'

The irony of the blind man leading her to safety wasn't lost on her, but she relaxed and followed his lead. He must have counted and logged his progress when they'd first entered because he guided them out of the cellar and up into the yard with relative ease. He closed the cellar door slowly to prevent the unsightly squeal of the hinges from alerting anyone to their presence.

Once the open air kissed her cheeks, Iona took a huge breath and relaxed her shoulders. It didn't matter that there were still many obstacles between their safe arrival at the cottage. At least they had escaped that horrid house and the equally dreadful woman within it. Royce grasped Iona's hand and they headed towards the cover of the shrubs that acted as a barrier from the winds of the loch.

Although they could still hear the men inside full

of grief and confusion over what the woman had done, they travelled on first through the yard and then down the same path to the shrubs and immense boulders that marked the path between the property and the sea. Soon, they were making their way down the same craggy rocks they had manoeuvred through before on their way to Webster's cottage.

'Let us get home,' Royce whispered, squeezing her hand as they rushed along.

Royce's use of the word *home* hadn't been lost on her. It made her heart flutter that he viewed the cottage as theirs and as a home. Or perhaps it was just an accident and a word used under duress. She bit her lip. It could well mean nothing at all.

The problem was she wanted it to. A thought that terrified her more than she wished to admit.

She wanted him to think of it as their home and for him to stay, but she also knew he was driven by a far greater purpose than love. He was bound by duty. She could see it in the way his body clenched and tightened when Webster had talked about his clan, his men and his family. It didn't matter that he didn't remember them. He was bound to them beyond memory. It was in his blood.

Or was it?

The woman's mention of one of them being 'tainted' still rang awkwardly in her head. It was an odd thing to say and had hit its mark in angering and confusing them, for such a thing couldn't be proven one way or another, could it? But it could prove divisive and pit one sibling against another if there was a question about legitimacy. Perhaps that was her plan all along in saying it and her goal was merely to set him on edge and against his siblings once he located them.

While the Camerons were a large clan set across several different places across the Highlands, all those places could be sent word until they discovered exactly which branch of such a clan he belonged to. Despite the risk they had taken in visiting Webster, it had served its purpose in finding some truth along with many other questions, but partial truth was far better than nothing at all. She only hoped Royce felt the same.

They had travelled the rest of the journey in silence, guided by the stars that had begun to peek out behind the clouds and the rhythmic tide of water rolling in against the shore. Once they reached the cottage, they entered quickly, dropped the latch and Iona flung herself around Royce, gripping him tightly to her.

She kissed him and he kissed her back swiftly before pulling away. His body was tight and tense as if ready to spring and he paced the small area before the hearth in silence. Even Jack could not win over his attention. After receiving love from Iona, the hound jumped back on to the mattress and laid down, his gaze following Royce's restless movements.

Not knowing what to do, Iona set about readying herself for bed. Despite her racing mind, her body ached with fatigue. She needed rest and so did he. She settled in next to Jack and pulled up the blanket to her chest.

'Royce, please rest. I do not wish for you to push yourself too hard.'

'Too hard?' he scoffed. 'I did not push hard enough this eve. She had one of my soldiers killed and tried to kill me. All in the name of keeping secrets related to my family, which I don't entirely understand, and now the crone is dead. And along with her goes my answers.'

He cursed and slammed his fist to the table, sending the bowls atop rattling from the force.

She started from his anger and stared up at him. She hadn't seen him this upset and agitated since the first day he had awoken in the cottage without his memory or sight. She lay silently in the bed, her heart racing in her chest.

Even Jack stared at Royce watchfully, as if he, too, was uncertain what the man would do next. Iona half expected him to bolt from the cottage and charge headlong back to Webster's home and try to shake the answers from her lifeless shell of a body. Thank the heavens he didn't.

He stripped off his shirt and trews and stood for a moment, staring out into the darkness. She studied his glorious naked form. All its muscled planes and slopes as if he were a piece of art himself. She smiled at the knowledge that he was hers.

Then she frowned. He was nothing of the sort. She only wished he were. She could not afford to believe otherwise. He came to the bed and she moved over to make room for him. He paused and felt for the extra blankets which she always left folded at the end of the mattress and took them before stretching one out on the floor before the fire. He settled down and covered himself with the other.

She swallowed the emotion clogging her throat and blinked back her tears. His silent rejection of her made her cheeks heat and her heart pound in her chest. What had she done? Or not done? Or was he merely distraught over Webster's passing and not having the answers he sought? Twice she opened her mouth to ask and twice she let her lips close back up to silence. She didn't know how to ask and she didn't know if she could handle the answer, so she curled up into the smallest ball she could and wept silently.

Royce knew he was a cad. Even now, he could hear the small hiccup coming from Iona's bed, but his anger and hatred of himself wouldn't allow him to move and comfort her. He didn't deserve to touch or hold her, and if he did, he knew he wouldn't be able to resist the sweet feel of her against his skin and the solace that her touch and another union with her would provide. He was a weak bastard who had let his man die and let the one blasted woman who had answers to the secrets he desired die before he got the truth from her.

All because he didn't want to risk Iona's life and because he feared losing her. His weakness and hesitation could have got them both killed. Despite his innate strength and skill, he'd stood there in the house addled and useless, which was the very man he had become since he'd been tossed headlong into the sea. And he hated himself for it more than he could put into words. He needed to leave here before he hurt Iona further and put her at even more risk.

If anyone had seen them travelling to Webster's house this eve her situation would be even more tenuous than it already was as she had no one to protect her, not even him. All he had done was cause her further exposure and possible exile from the only home she had ever known by staying in her cottage…and made her believe he could offer her something, such as a life with him.

When he'd taken her virginity, he knew the promise he was making to her and he'd been sure he could provide her a life, but now, a mere day later, he realised what a fool he was. That was what happened when a man thought with his cock rather than his head. He ran a hand down his face and turned on to his back.

Iona's hiccups subsided and he hoped it meant she had fallen asleep and had some reprieve from the disappointment he had brought upon her. If only this bloody eternal darkness would subside and his memory would return. Until it did, all he would cause her was more misery. And even if he did recover his memory and his sight, would she come with him to begin a life elsewhere back at his clan if he asked her? He knew he couldn't stay, but would she be willing to leave this place that had always been her home?

These were all things he should have thought of… yesterday before he'd bedded her. Now, he was just an arse.

He closed his eyes and released a long breath. And

then there was who he was. Now that he knew, or at least largely suspected, that he was a laird of Clan Cameron, he could begin the daunting task of figuring out which branch of the clan he was from in the Highlands and where he had come from. And once he discovered that, he could determine if anything Webster had said was true about one of the siblings being tainted, or at least try to.

Chapter Eighteen

Iona woke with scratchy, puffy eyes and a general ache to her body. Faint sunlight streamed into her windows as the sun rose in the east. Jack's head rested across her stomach and he flicked his gaze up at her as if he, too, was uncertain about how the day would go. She patted his head and smiled down at him. Even if she lost everything and everyone, she would still have Jack.

Royce slept in front of the hearth even though the fire had long gone out, his chest rising and falling peacefully. He looked like a boy, with his face relaxed and his features peaceful. She shivered as she stared down at his fine form and realised how empty this cottage and her life would be without him. But he had made his position clear without any words at all when he chose to sleep on the floor last night. Her heart squeezed in her chest and she felt the scar along her cheek.

She'd been fooling herself, hadn't she? She was destined to be alone. She was the recluse, the sea witch, and solitude suited her and protected her. Further loss was not to be borne. It was why she'd chosen to stay here out on the shore's edge, far away from town. Such solitude had worked for her father and protected him from further grief, and it would work for her. She just needed to focus on what she needed to do to raise enough funds to pay back Chisholm before he reclaimed the cottage as his own.

Perhaps Webster's death would distract him for a week or so while all the preparations were taken care of. As the elder male heir, he would oversee making such arrangements for her funeral and no doubt find a way to collect his quarter of the island as quickly as possible.

Iona could only hope there was a dispute instigated by her sons to keep her lands and home for themselves, even if they had little grounds for such a complaint. Extra time was all Iona needed. She cared not exactly how she got it.

She shifted to get up and see if any new requests had been delivered to her box last eve since she hadn't checked properly. She readied herself, completed her ablutions, then she and Jack headed outside. The fresh air felt glorious on her face. Although she smelled the storm on the wind, the blue skies with a smattering of fluffy clouds promised a day of sun before the storm rolled in this evening.

Ambling to the small box, she found herself smiling and humming a tune despite herself. She would be fine on her own. She knew that. And at least they would have had one lovely night together. A memory to keep her warm during the quiet solitary nights ahead. She might even be able to enjoy her remaining time with him and help him solve this odd riddle regarding his family.

She gathered the collection of notes from the box and headed back to the cottage. Royce was outside near the barn, patiently feeling his way for the latch. She paused and watched him. He was a far cry from the restless man of last night and the desperate man from the first night he woke after his injuries.

He found the food and sprinkled it on the ground for the goats and chickens that rallied around him. He talked to them as he worked just as she did. If she didn't know better, she would have thought him... content.

'They are hungry this morn,' he said, not even glancing back at her.

'How did you know I was here?' she asked.

'Lucky guess.'

She frowned, knowing it was much more than that, but it was no matter. 'I will prepare something to break our fast.'

'Aye. I will come in once I am done with these chores.'

She smiled despite herself. He had become quite self-sufficient over the last week. He had learned his surroundings and begun to sense others and hear their arrival. Even if he did not fully regain his faculties, he could survive and defend himself...to a point. Would he be able to continue as laird? She bit her lip.

Nay. No clan would allow what they believed to

be a weak figurehead to lead their people. Too much instability rested among them. While Lismore was largely protected from such power struggles, the mainland was not. When he returned, it would be a struggle for him to remain in power.

She prayed his sight would return and his memories not far behind it. The sooner he knew who he was and returned to his life, the better off they would both be. She entered the cottage and set aside the requests from the box, so she could start a fire and cook some fresh eggs to break their fast.

Soon, the eggs were cooked, and the aroma filled the air. Her stomach rumbled as she set their plates on the table. Royce entered and joined her. They ate in an awkward silence and quickly cleaned their plates. She rose to start the dishes and Royce reached out and gripped her wrist.

'I am sorry,' he said quietly.

His simple words hung in the air between them and her eyes welled.

'I am, too,' she answered.

While they might not have even been speaking of the same thing, it didn't matter. She was sorry they would have to part. Sorry he couldn't see. Sorry Webster had died before he gleaned his truth. She was sorry for a great deal many things. But despite it all she could never be sorry for him, for what they shared, even if it was a fleeting, fragile thing that wouldn't last.

He ran his thumb over the inside of her wrist once,

then twice, and a shiver ran along her skin. She bit her lip so she didn't sigh aloud.

It seemed Royce had set a simmering fire within her that could be ignited with minimal touch. She held her breath and finally he released her wrist slowly as if he was painfully reluctant to do so.

Her body hummed from his touch and she took a moment to collect herself before she carried on. The dishes landed on the counter with a chaotic clatter. She closed her eyes and leaned on the counter, trying to regain her emotional balance. The man could undo her with a mere touch to her wrist and she hated it.

He cleared his throat and went to her. He stood behind her, his hand on the small of her back. 'Let me,' he said, gently guiding her out of the way and taking the dishes from her. 'What tinctures are we making today?'

She watched him struggle to clean the dishes at first, but soon he had an ease to his movements. She gathered the notes and opened them. 'One for megrim, another for a salve for a rash and…'

I saw ye. I know he is there.

She covered her mouth with her hand. The words were cast in various sizes on the page and the writing was effortful. Whoever penned it did not write often. Ink had bled through in heavy circles where they had hesitated, perhaps unsure of how to form the next letter. Either way the meaning was quite clear.

They knew Royce was with her.

'Iona?' Royce asked, setting the last plate on the rack to dry.

'Someone knows you are here.'

He stilled and stared. 'What? How can you be so sure?'

'Someone put a note in my box. It says, *"I saw ye. I know he is there."* The meaning is unmistakable.'

'Aye,' he agreed. 'It is. What shall we do about it?'

She shrugged. 'I do not know. I cannot tell who wrote it by the hand and anyone could have dropped it within the box. And they may be bluffing. They may know nothing and just be trying to scare me.'

'Or they could know everything and this is their way of threatening you. Is there anything else identifying about it?'

She flipped it over and scanned it. 'Other than it being a bit yellowed from age, I cannot see anything of note.'

'May I?' he asked, extending his hand to her.

She set the letter in his palm, careful not to touch him lest her body flare up with longing once more.

He took it and felt the weight of it. 'It is heavier than the others. Perhaps it is older if it is more dense parchment.' He brought it to his nose and sniffed. 'There is some odour to it that I recognise. What is it?' He pinched the bridge of his nose. 'I cannot place it. Can you?' he asked, extending his hand to her.

She sniffed the paper. 'Ah, I do recognise it. Butterwort. 'Tis a foul-smelling plant. I can't think of a tincture I have made with it, but it is quite common on the isle. Perhaps someone else uses it to make their tinctures. They say it aids respiratory ailments.'

'Now we need to locate a person with a respiratory ailment,' he teased and set it aside.

'That could be almost anyone,' she said.

'Well, think about it. You know more about people than you even realise. You make their tinctures. You know what ails them and what their bodies' weaknesses are. That is a powerful tool whether you realise it or not.'

She paused. 'You are right. I have never thought about it in that way. I will think upon it while we prepare these. Hopefully my busy hands will help my mind hone in on the person responsible for this note.'

Chapter Nineteen

Royce woke to a sharp, throbbing pain in his head. He winced and felt the knot on the side of his head before draping his arm over his eyes, not daring to open them just yet. Yesterday had been a disaster to be sure, but somehow, he failed to remember being throttled in the head. The last thing he remembered was hearing Chisholm speaking to Iona outside. What had happened after that?

He let his arm fall away and opened his eyes to embrace the darkness that always followed. But today, it wasn't blackness that greeted him, but murky colours. He blinked to clear the foggy shapes and colours before him. A thatched ceiling came into focus and then sunlight streamed in through a solitary window in the cottage.

The cottage.

He could see.

His heart surged in his chest, his pulse picked up speed and he blinked again for fear he was dreaming or his vision temporary.

It wasn't. He could see.

Despite his desire to charge from the bed, he sat up slowly, not wanting to jostle his sight as if any rapid movement could seize his vision away once more. Had his head injury from last night caused his sight to return?

Did it even matter? He could see.

He leaned back on his elbows and took in the sight around him. His headache receded as he rejoiced in his surroundings. Jack, who turned out to be an older, dark, wiry hound with a greying beard, stared at him, his tongue lolling out the side of his mouth. Royce revelled in the sight of the beloved hound who had kept him company in so many ways and rubbed the dog's head. After having his fill of attention, Jack jumped down from the bed.

In so many ways the cottage was exactly as he had imagined. The walls were whitewashed, the grey stone hearth sat upon the opposite wall and the home itself was tidy, warm and inviting. The wooden table and chairs where he and Iona had shared much time together were worn, but well-tended, and the counter was arranged neatly with carved bowls, plates, pots and herbs, along with the stone mortar and pestle he had used so often. A small vase with a colourful spray of blue and white flowers rested on the table near him. The home was cared for and loved, just as he had been by Iona.

Iona.

His gaze sought her out, his body hungry for the sight of her, his desire to see her in the quiet of sleep outweighing the need to shout aloud and call out to her that he had regained his vision. His body tensed at the sight of her curled under a gathering of plaid blankets on the floor, selflessly sparing her bed for him once more, no doubt due to his injury. Her long wavy black hair was loose and streaming down the middle of her back in long tendrils and a few of them framed her face.

His chest tightened. Her face.

Glory be, she was beautiful. Far more so than he could have ever imagined. Long dark lashes rested upon her fair face and her pert nose and smooth simple lips were perfect for her delicate features. Even her scarred cheek was beautiful, a part of her that she had dared share with him. Its dark purple ridges were a testament to her strength and ability to survive all alone here.

He mustered his courage and rose from the bed. Jack beckoned to be let out and Royce opened the door, staring out at the glorious isle that was Lismore. After soaking in the fresh air for a few breaths, he returned to Iona.

What did one say to the woman who had saved his life and spared all for him now that he could look her in the eyes and thank her properly? His pulse raced. He knelt by her side, and ran a shaky hand down her cheek, his thumb caressing her temple and then sliding back into her silky hair.

'Iona,' he said softly, unable to keep the urgency from his voice. He could wait no longer to share his happiness with her. She had brought him back to life and he wanted to see her face when he told her he'd finally regained his sight.

Her eyes fluttered open and her magnificent moss-green irises arrested his attention. He gazed at them in awe, studying the different shades of green and the tiny flecks of blue nestled within them, like blue birds flying across a glen.

'Good morning,' he murmured. 'You are so beautiful,' he said, his voice cracking from the emotion flooding him at the sight of her staring back at him.

She stilled. 'You can see me?' she asked, sitting up slowly.

'Aye.'

'It is a miracle,' she said, smiling at him.

'Aye,' he said, his eyes filling. 'And you are the most glorious creature I have ever seen. I could not imagine just how much so. Look at you,' he murmured. He clutched her face, soaking in every feature.

She gripped his hands that cupped her face and tried to look away, no doubt self-conscious from his acute appraisal of her. 'Royce, I am no such thing. You are merely joyful at regaining your sight.'

'Nay,' he countered. 'Look at me.' He waited for her to meet his gaze, noting her eyes filling with tears. 'Iona MacKenzie,' he said, his voice breaking. 'You. Are. Beautiful.'

She shook her head. 'I am but scarred and ugly.' A tear spilled down her cheek.

'Nay. You are the most beautiful woman I have ever seen. I love your scar. It is a testament to who you are. Your strength, courage and love.' He ran his thumb over it, and she shivered. He leaned in slowly, letting his lips hover in the air in anticipation of what a kiss with her would be now that he could see her. Now that he felt he might have something in this world to offer her other than being an added burden.

His lips reached hers and the moment of contact sent a surge of intense heat and desire through him. A flash of memory of the feel of her flesh beneath him the night they had made love seized him. She clutched his bare back, her fingertips running along the ridge of his spine, and he gasped into her mouth and seized her lips once more in a hungry and urgent kiss.

His hands wove into her hair and their kisses deepened until he feared he might well drown in his feelings for her, pulled under by the emotion and desire flooding him now that he felt like he was a real, complete man again, able to care and love and provide for her.

She shifted against his torso and he tugged away the blanket between them. His palms skimmed every part of her he could reach—her neck, collarbone, the soft slope of her shoulders—but it wasn't enough. He needed to see her, every ivory rise and fall of her body. He slid his hand under her shift and revelled in the feel of his hand on her and the hitch in her breath. Snatching his lips away, he stared upon her face, the delicate pink in her cheeks and the slight widening of the pupils in her eyes.

'I want…' he said, his voice raspy. He wanted so many things that he didn't know where to begin. To provide for her, care for her, share a life with her, make love to her...

'I want you, too,' she whispered back with a soft feathery touch to his lips.

'I want that as well, but I want to give you everything, Iona,' he whispered. 'I want to share my life with you and my future with you.'

'Shh... Let us just be with one another now and not worry over the future,' she replied, rising to her knees. She lifted the shift over her head and off her in one deft movement that made Royce lose all thought and reason. His throat dried at the sight of her naked body before him. The soft smooth mounds of her breasts and the small rosy buds of her nipples were perfection. His gaze roved down to the tiny belly button and the dark triangle of hair between her shapely legs.

This woman was offering herself to him. Again. 'I do not deserve you, Iona,' he replied. 'But I will endeavour to, day after day after day,' he murmured. 'If you will have me.'

Iona moaned in pleasure. While she knew this would be a goodbye, rather than the beginning of their future that he expressed, she would revel in it none the less. Royce sucked on her breast and she clutched his head to her chest, unable to cease the raw pleasure of his touch from hurtling through her body like a storm raging along the sky. She had promised Chisholm her cottage in exchange for Royce's safety and such an exchange she would never regret. Just like their love making now and exchange of souls she would never regret.

She would cherish it for ever.

Royce's hands drifted down her torso as he suckled, gripping her hips and pulling them against his groin. His manhood strained against his trews and she could feel that she was not the only one pining for their union.

He lifted his head and seized her mouth, his tongue capturing her own as he guided her back to the floor. Then he lifted his lips from her own and flashed her a wicked smile. 'I have imagined you, Iona, but my imagination failed me. You are exquisite and I shall linger over every part of you to show you. Shall I begin?'

She giggled and ran her fingertips along his brow. 'Only if I can do the same in return.'

He nodded. 'Although I venture to say you may be too tired after I am through with you.' He winked and pressed a kiss between her breasts before making his way slowly down her belly. Soon, his lips were on her core and she gasped, her hips lifting involuntarily from the exquisite feel of his mouth there.

'Steady, my love,' he murmured, caressing her thighs with his palms as he kissed her intimately.

She sank into the folds of the blankets, her head arching back as she closed her eyes at the pleasure his mouth gave her. The coil of heat heightened in her and the tight pressure became unbearable. 'Royce,' she pleaded. 'It feels too heavenly. I cannot bear it.' He increased the intensity of his kisses. Then, she gasped at the riotous explosion of sensation as it cascaded through her body.

She panted and opened her eyes to see him above her staring down at her face with contentment. 'You are even more beautiful when you are pleasured,' he said, trailing a finger along her jawline.

Her cheeks heated and she leaned into his touch. 'Such pleasure I have never had before. You are gifted in the art of lovemaking.'

He lifted his brow. 'We have only just begun,' he said, pressing light kisses to her cheek, and turned her on her side.

'Your trews, my laird. You cannot deny me the feel of you against my flesh.' She frowned.

He stood, stripped and joined her under the blanket before she could utter another word. The feel of him made her gasp and sigh all in the same breath.

'Now where were we?' he asked, nibbling on the back of her ear as his hand wrapped around her waist.

'I believe you were about to ravage me with your lovemaking skills, my laird.'

'Aye. I was, wasn't I?' he replied, the feel of his smile upon her neck.

Chapter Twenty

Royce yawned and rolled to his side. Had he ever been more sated or happier? Iona slept, her face resting on his chest. Jack snoozed in front of the fire Royce had built between bouts of lovemaking with Iona, and the sunset was building layers of orange, pinks and reds across the sky. His head had begun a dull ache, but he'd not complain. He could see and he had the woman he loved in his arms. He stilled as the thought popped unbidden in his head.

He *did* love her.

The truth of it no longer paralysed him because he could care for her properly now…if he was free to do so. The thought that he might not be free plagued him. He could see and he had an inkling of who he was now, but nothing about the inner workings of his life as his memory had not returned. It reminded him that he needed to ask Iona what had happened from the night before that had caused such a blow to his head. He might need to thank the bastard who hit him for accidentally restoring his vision.

Throughout the day, he'd meant to ask her, but each time they had fallen back into an embrace and he was unable to focus on anything other than the smooth, warm feel of her flesh against his palms. Even now, his body buzzed as he ran his calloused fingertips along her bare back.

If only his memory would return. Then, he could ask for her hand and bring her back to wherever it was he resided on the mainland. He could be the husband and laird he longed to be with the woman he loved by his side and they could raise a brood of beautiful sons and daughters with Iona's heart and mind and his stubbornness. He smiled at that thought. Their children would be a force to be reckoned with.

The thought of waiting until his memory returned made his skin itch. Why did he have to wait? What if she loved him enough now to say yes without even knowing who he really was? His fingertips stilled. What if she didn't?

He cared not to think upon that possibility. Not at all. As if sensing his internal struggle, she shifted against him and opened her eyes, peering up at him full of drowsy wonder.

'Good morn?' she asked.

'Nay. 'Tis a good eve. The sun is setting,' he answered, nodding towards the sky and its blooming colours.

'Then we can stay abed. I am pleased with such an idea, although I must complete my chores.' She hid her face in his chest and her unruly hair flopped forward dramatically. He couldn't help but laugh and ruffle her wild waves further.

'I can help. I can do them blind, you know,' he teased.

She groaned against his flesh. 'Have you been waiting all day to say that?'

'Perhaps. I find sight has gifted me a sense of humour and light-heartedness I did not possess before. Do you agree?'

She rested her chin on his chest and scrutinised him. 'You may be right. I have not seen a scowl all day.' She furrowed her brow. 'Who are you?' she teased. He pulled her up to his lap and she laughed, smiling at him.

'I am the Laird you saved at sea and brought back to life. The one who has tried to show his affection and appreciation for you all day.' He paused, his heart feeling reckless and heavy. He tucked her hair behind her perfect petite earlobe. 'I am the man who wishes to spend all of my days with you, if you will have me.'

Her gaze searched his, some uncertainty reflected in her irises. 'What?' she asked.

'I want you to marry me, Iona. To come with me to wherever it is I come from. To build a life with me. To build a glorious future together.'

She bit her lip and shifted off his lap. 'Royce, you have suffered a head injury. You have had the shock of regaining your sight. You cannot make such a decision so hastily. You may wake tomorrow and…' She didn't complete the sentence, but Royce knew what she intended.

Change his mind. Or he might be blind again or regain his memories.

He did not know his future, which made this moment even more precious to him.

She looked away and covered herself. 'To make such a promise before you even know who you are is a house built on sand with the tide coming in.'

The logical side of him knew she was right. She was being sensible, but he wanted to do anything but be sensible. He loved her and he'd never loved a woman in all his life.

He scratched his head.

Or at least he didn't *think* he had.

Blast. He scrubbed a hand down his face. He was making her point for her.

'What happened last night?' he asked, hoping knowing what had caused him injury might help further his cause somehow.

'What do you remember?' she replied.

'I remember being here at the cottage with you and Jack, Jack barking to alert us to a noise outside and then hearing Chisholm had stopped by to speak with you. I was concerned with his tone, he sounded loud and angry, so I went outside and joined you. That is the last of it.'

Her shoulders relaxed. 'That is the most important bit of it, I suppose. The other detail is that he didn't come alone. He brought Webster's sons.'

'Why?'

'It turns out they believed you had poisoned their mother with some tincture of mine to be rid of her because of your mysterious family secrets she referenced. It was Webster who scrawled the note to us. She had told her sons of her belief you were here with me, even though she had not actually seen you. The boys delivered the note to my box before they went into town for drinks. We did not see them because we were breaking into their house at the time.' She cringed. 'They didn't take kindly to that part of the story when I relayed it to them.'

'And?'

'And what?'

'Surely more happened after that?'

'Chisholm kindly reminded me of my need to repay him for the loan on my cottage,' she said, 'so I gave what little else I had scrounged up to him and he went on his way.'

'He went on his way? Just like that? And Webster's sons left as well when they originally believed I killed their mother?' He frowned. Iona wasn't telling him something.

'More or less,' she answered, coyly looking down at her hands.

'What did I do? Surely I did not just stand there like a dolt and do nothing.'

She shook her head. 'Aye. You did something. You started a row with them.'

He nodded. Now they were getting somewhere in the story. That sounded more like something he would do. 'Over what?' he asked.

'Your soldier. The one they killed.' She stared back at him then, meeting his gaze.

His throat tightened. 'His name?'

'Athol. Seems he was your most trusted warrior from what they remember you saying about him. They killed him when you would not agree to come alone to see Webster.'

He clenched his jaw. 'Why did they not just kill me then?' he asked pointedly. 'Wasn't that the whole point of their visit—to avenge the death of their mother that they believed I caused?'

'Aye. Perhaps at first it was. They were quite angry and out of sorts with grief.' Her words withered in the air and died away.

He clutched her hand. 'And why did that not happen?'

'We made an arrangement,' she offered, looking away from him.

He tilted her chin towards him. 'Of what sort?' he asked. His gut churned and his heart tripped over itself, his instincts roiling and screaming aloud that he would not like what she said next. He didn't need sight to know it either. He could feel it in the slight tremor of her hand and the rapid pulse at the base of her wrist.

Still, she didn't answer.

'Iona?' he said. 'Please. Tell me what you have done.'

She lifted her face to him and the agony in her eyes sent alarm through him. 'I…' she said. 'I agreed to give them the cottage, all the animals save Jack, and what meagre belongings I had in exchange for your safe return home. They agreed.'

His body chilled. She had given up all she had in the world for him.

* * *

Of all the responses Iona had anticipated, silence hadn't been one of them. She watched Royce and the stillness of his body relayed his shock. She'd almost not told him, but this newfound freedom she felt in telling the truth and in making choices gave her joy. Aiding his safe return to his people was the right decision. She knew that even if he didn't.

Finally, he blinked and let go of her hand. He rose, tugged on his trews and went to the window. He stared out for long minutes his arm outstretched, leaning on the frame of the window, his form filling almost the entire pane. His body was a dark silhouette against the sunset's riotous colours. Once again, he was a glorious wolf against the world, exactly as he should be, unhindered and free.

And that meant free of her, too.

'Why?' he asked, his voice low, still staring out at the loch as the last curved edge of the sun dipped down into the sea. 'Why would you give up all you have in this world to save me?'

'Because I am a mere healer and you are a laird. You can do great things with your power. Your people need you.'

'And what of you?' he said, a tightness in his voice as he turned to face her.

'Me?' she asked, uncertain of his question and the anger that laced his words.

'Aye,' he replied. 'What of you? You agreed to such an arrangement before I proposed to you this morn.

What were you planning? To ship me off in the night once you located my family?'

She squirmed.

'Bloody hell,' he cursed. 'You were.'

'You make it seem like a horrid piece of trickery, but it was not. I did it to save you. I was never going to have enough money to save this cottage, you know that,' she answered, hurt by his words and the accusation that she had done something wrong by preserving his future.

'I could have…' he replied and then stopped.

'You could have what?' she replied. 'Fought them off? There were three of them, Royce. Three men, me and Jack. We could have all ended up dead. If only your pride would allow you to acknowledge that I did what I had to do for all our sakes.' She threw off the blanket that had been covering her and stood before him naked, her hair wild and tousled, and in desperate need of a comb. She didn't care. Not any more.

He just stared at her, his eyes roving over every inch of her as if he were memorising her now in this moment. The connection they had had all day seemed severed and they stood as strangers. All because she had given him something he did not want. She'd given him a life without her. She'd given him his freedom.

Chapter Twenty-One

Royce wanted to run out to the pebbly shore of the loch and roar. Just when he had his sight returned and believed he could have a life with Iona, she had all but rejected him in some vain attempt to save him. He felt as he had that first day on Lismore. Once again, he was the blind man on the shore who woke and hadn't wished to be saved. But it wasn't too late to undo what she had done. He could charge into town and undo all of it.

But first he needed to know her answer.

He needed to know if she had done this because she loved him or because she did not love him. Or for a far more sinister reason: fear.

'Why did you truly do this?' he murmured.

She blinked back at him and shook her head. 'Because I wanted to help you, save you, and return you to the life you deserve. While you may not have found out the whole truth about your family, you are a laird and still have a family and clan of people to return to and care for.'

She picked up her shift and slid it over her body. For a moment he was arrested by the way the thin fabric slid along her curves so effortlessly, just as her limbs had fit so perfectly against his own mere minutes before.

'Do I frighten you? Does the idea of being with me terrify you that much more than being alone that you would go to such extremes to keep my love at bay?' he asked, his words laced with accusation and disappointment.

She froze like a deer when it feels the gaze of its predator upon them. In that moment, he knew he'd hit his mark. His words had struck the truth like an arrow.

He felt ill.

She shifted on her feet and gathered the rumpled morning dress from the floor and slipped into it. On the second button, she stopped, her gaze hitting him full on, her green eyes bright and wild. 'You think you know me so well?' she challenged. 'You believe I wilfully put an obstacle between us to keep myself here and alone?'

He took several steps towards her and reached out his hand to run his fingertips along her scar, its purple ridges darkening under the blush heating of her cheeks. 'Aye. I do. It is too scary a thing to risk your beloved life of solitude and control. I should know, I believe I was the same.'

'How would you know?' she said angrily.

Her words stung him hard and he let his hand fall away.

'You are right,' he scoffed, unable to keep the bitterness from his voice. 'I only know what my gut tells me. I have few memories to guide me, unlike you who is living within your memories alone.'

She opened her lips to say something and stopped.

'Isn't that the truth? The past and fear drive you to remain here. Why else would you wish to stay here on this island anyway? You describe to me places like the ruins of St Moluag and Tirefour Castle in such beauty and detail, but you do not allow yourself the pleasure of visiting them any more. All because you fear what others will think of you and your scar or do not wish to be reminded of your losses.

'What if no one cares about your scars, Iona? What if you walked into town and no one gave you a second glance? What if everyone wanted to know you and you had to risk a connection with them? Would you be happy or sad?'

'How dare you speak to me such!' she shouted.

'Why shouldn't I? 'Tis the truth, isn't it? You are too scared to risk loving and caring for anyone. Too scared to lose anyone else. Is that not the real reason you are in this cottage all alone by the shore, caring for the lost and wounded? There is no risk of attachment here.'

'That is not true. I am needed here. I am a healer. It is what I do and who I am. And this…this is the only home I know.' Her voice cracked with emotion and it nearly undid his resolve to stay where he was. Part of him wished to run to her and kiss her and tell her he didn't mean a word of it. The other part of him knew every word he said was a truth she needed to hear.

And a truth he needed to hear as well.

She didn't want him, or at least not enough to leave, and the realisation of it cut him deeply.

'You…' he said quietly and then cleared his throat. 'You are a reminder of why I should focus on being laird. Risking anything else is perilous at best.' He grabbed his shirt, coat and boots and headed to the door.

'Where are you going?' she called.

'To town. I care not who sees me or what they say. I must try to find out more about my father's secrets, whether Webster's sons and Chisholm try to kill me or not. Hiding here will not solve anything. Of all people, *you* should know that.'

He yanked the door open and slammed it shut.

And as much as he wished to deny it, as he headed along the beach, he was half listening and hoping for the sound of the cottage door to open and for Iona to call out his name.

Iona thought about running after him, but her feet were heavy blocks of uncertainty. Minutes had passed and she hadn't moved from within the centre of the cottage. His words still stung her and echoed dully in her head.

''Tis the truth, isn't it? You are too scared to risk loving and caring for anyone. Too scared to lose anyone else. Is that not the real reason you are in this cottage all alone by the shore, caring for the lost and wounded? There is no risk of attachment here.'

She clutched the fabric of her gown to keep her

hands from trembling even more than they already were. Her eyes welled. A part of her knew he might be right, while the other part of her hated him and rejected the words for their cruelty. How could he be so angry at her for giving him his life back, so he could fulfil his destiny as laird and provide for his people? She'd earned him safe passage away from here, an isle he would never return to once he left anyway. She didn't expect him to give up his future for her. She was setting him free as she did all healed things.

Freedom was a gift.

Wasn't it?

But it was also one she dared not give herself. While she had sacrificed the cottage and animals she loved as she had no other choice and it would spare him, she wasn't giving up her plans to stay on the isle and continue as a healer. She would simply have to find a different means of doing such and a place for her and Jack to live. This was what she was meant to do. If she didn't carry on the tradition as healer here on the isle, what would she be? And what would happen to the memory of her parents?

Her throat dried.

They would be gone for ever, as if they had never existed in the first place. She swallowed hard. And if she dared leave here…she couldn't begin to think beyond these shores. She rested her hand on her scarred cheek and her face heated. How would others treat her? At least here, she was ignored for the most part, which was a far better thing than to be mocked and ridiculed by strangers.

She squared her shoulders, her resolve settling in further. Nay, she would never leave Lismore. This was her home and it always would be. It didn't matter what Royce thought. He could never understand. How could he? As a man and laird, the world bent to his whim, whereas she, as a single woman of little means, had to wrestle it into submission.

She frowned. And the outcomes were not always favourable.

Jack barked outside, snatching her back from her musings, and she couldn't help but smile.

As always, Jack saved her from herself. She walked outside and busied herself with the many chores that needed to be tended to. Rather than rushing through them this eve, she savoured them, knowing her days of lingering along the barn while listening to the birds call out over the sea waters were now numbered. She mucked the barn and put down some new hay and tossed out some feed for the goats and chickens. Her favourite baby goat nuzzled its small budding horns against her leg and she stopped to pull the tiny creature into her lap.

'What say you to a new home?' she cooed and he let out a little bah of approval.

Iona was no fool. She knew most of her animals would have to find new homes as the future was an uncertain one. But perhaps Chisholm would find a new tenant who wished to care for them as she did and only she and Jack would be displaced. Either way, there would be change, one of the things she despised most in this world.

* * *

After she had finished her chores, she washed up and went inside. She prepared a pot of stew and set it over the newly lit fire in the hearth. Jack snuggled up near the door and, for the first time in a long time, Iona didn't wish to swim. The waters looked dark and still, much like how she felt as she moved about the cottage that looked so large and empty without Royce in it.

'What do you think he is up to, Jack?' she asked her beloved hound as she stared out at the dark horizon. It was hard to imagine him wandering through Lismore at night in hopes of finding answers. She gathered a bowl and spoon and set them at the table, the solitary setting for her meal another odd adjustment to the eve.

The firelight caught the polished sheen of Catriona's face on the brooch Royce had neglected to take with him. Iona picked it up and rubbed her fingers across it. He hadn't even had a chance to look upon it this morn after he had regained his sight. What if he had looked upon it and recognised her instantly? Then both of them would have at least some of the answers they sought.

For a moment, she was tempted to throw on her cloak and traverse through the shadows of town in search of him, but then discarded such a foolhardy thought. If he wanted it, he would return for it, wouldn't he? Just as if he wanted to speak with her again before he left the isle, he would return as well, no matter how unlikely such a thought seemed.

'I suppose it is just you and I again, Jack,' Iona murmured setting the brooch back on that table.

Just as she always thought it would be.

Chapter Twenty-Two

The terrain was not nearly as treacherous now that Royce could see. His body even remembered some of the shoreline from their previous travels to Webster's home; his boots gripped the rock and sands as he climbed the hillside in the direction of town. It also didn't seem quite as enjoyable alone.

He opened and closed his hand, the longing to have Iona's palm clutching his making a part of his body ache. He was a lovesick fool and he despised himself for it. Such a distraction would get him killed if he wasn't careful. He was heading into a town where some of the men wanted him dead. He needed to focus on his surroundings and uncovering the truth of the secrets he came to the island to gather in the first place.

At least the moon aided his progress. It was full and bright, casting shadows as well as light through the fog building after the sun had melted into the horizon. It provided coverage as well as guidance as to what homes and people were ahead. He also hoped the wet ground would grant him the provided grace of not warning others of his approach until he was ready to reveal himself.

He smiled when he spied the ruins of the church of St Moluag that Iona had described to him in such intricate detail and affection. Its grey stone walls climbed unevenly up to the night sky and its partial roof let in scatterings of moonlight, giving it a haunting and romantic appearance. No wonder she adored it.

Soon, he saw the first row of headstones in the nearby cemetery and he faltered, wondering which ones harboured her parents. He shook his head. He needed to focus on the task ahead. Thinking about Iona and her cares would only distract him. Setting it aside until he had the proper time to grieve his disappointment was the safest and wisest of decisions for now.

Even if his heart told him otherwise. It was his heart that had got him in this bloody mess, so Royce would do well to ignore it…for now at least.

He climbed another hill and a modest row of shops came into view. Two appeared to be still open. Candles flickered from within them, giving the windows a warm glow. The noise from each one filtered out into the street as the doors to each opened and closed when patrons went in and out. As he expected, they were the local inns and they would serve as the best place for him to garner answers, but they also harboured great danger, for he didn't know who was friend or foe by sight, but by voice alone.

He rolled his neck, squared his shoulders and

checked the small blade that was tucked within his trews and hidden beneath his jacket. It wasn't much, but it was something. He could only hope his instincts and gut could do the rest. His gaze clicked up to the sign outside his first stop, The Laughing Goat Inn, and he nodded at the irony. It seemed the perfect place to start.

Entering the inn, Royce immediately realised his mistake: he was a stranger. All gazes clicked up to him as they would upon anyone coming in, but since he was unknown to everyone, the gazes held and scrutinised him rather than falling back to their tankards or companions. A few of the men sat up in their chairs, their brows furrowing, disapproval etched openly on their features.

Deuces.

He clearly hadn't thought this all the way through, but it was also too late to turn back now. He had been seen. *Acknowledge the enemy.* The advice popped into his head unbidden and Royce decided to trust it. He approached the table full of men who appeared the most threatened by his presence. If he won them over, the rest of the inn would fall into submission. However, if he didn't, then his search for answers would be quite short lived.

But at least he would have tried. There would be no more wondering or hiding.

'Good eve,' he said, towering over them as they sat, his attempt to make himself appear as large and formidable as possible.

They stared back at him and the oldest at the table responded, 'Aye. What brings ye here, stranger?'

The man's voice didn't register in Royce's memory and he felt a flicker of disappointment.

'A search for information. I'm looking for Chisholm as well as Webster's sons.'

At the mention of the men's names, more of the inn grew quiet and two of the men at the table before him shifted in their chairs. Another set down his tankard. 'Who wants to know?' another man asked from the table behind.

Royce almost smiled. It was Chisholm. He'd recognise the man's voice anywhere. He clutched one of his fists at his side as a flash of memory of the man's ugly exchange with Iona came to the forefront of his mind.

'Ah, Chisholm. I had hoped to find you here.'

The older man's eyes widened for the briefest of moments, reflecting his surprise at being challenged, and then his gaze narrowed in on Royce. Perhaps the light had disguised Royce's features momentarily, but now he could see Chisholm recognised him as well.

'Cameron,' he replied, the note of irritation in his voice evident as he splayed his palm flat to the table. 'I thought we had come to an understanding that you would leave without incident and as soon as you were able.'

'Nay. That was an agreement made with Miss MacKenzie. It was not made with me. I prefer to tend to my own affairs. Whatever agreement was made is now void. You will discuss new terms with me. Now, preferably.'

The man frowned and rose from his chair. Two younger men beside him rose in tandem and Royce almost felt giddy at the sight of it. Webster's sons, no doubt. He had stumbled upon all the men he sought in one fell swoop. It seemed luck was on his side this eve.

It was about bloody time his luck turned for the better.

The inn fell nearly silent except for the shifting of patrons in their chairs and the errant clanging of pots and pans from the kitchen in the back. Evidently, Chisholm wasn't prone for hasty decision making and he stood assessing Royce while Webster's sons stood patiently by his side.

'Come,' he finally replied. He drained the remnants of his tankard of ale and slammed it back on the table. 'While I believe you will regret your decision to re-negotiate the terms of your stay, I believe in allowing all men to create their own failings.' Webster's sons snickered.

Royce frowned but did not react. The insult was but the first play in a very long game with the man for a prize Royce desperately needed to win: the truth. He also knew his actions might very well impact Iona's future, so he would tread carefully for as long as he could until he had a clearer picture of what exactly was happening on this small isle. His gut told him that he was only seeing a very small corner of a large, complicated puzzle.

'Bobby, can we take the back room for our…discussion?' Chisholm asked, still glaring at Royce.

The stout, red-faced barman ceased wiping down a table in the corner. 'Aye. Remember, whatever ye break, ye buy.'

Webster's sons snickered again and Royce commanded himself not to roll his eyes. They were dullards and would only complicate the process of gaining information from Chisholm.

'Could we leave this arrangement between the two of us?' Royce shifted his weight on his feet. ''Tis the least you can do after what they did to my companion.'

'Nay,' one of the young men answered. 'Ye will answer for what ye did to our mother.'

The other began to chime in as well. Chisholm lifted a hand to cease their whining and they fell silent.

'Wait here,' he told them without his gaze leaving Royce's own.

They started to object, but ceased and returned to their chairs, sending their feeble attempts at a withering glance Royce's way. Ignoring them, Royce followed Chisholm into the back room and settled at a table.

'I respect your nerve in coming here, but little else,' Chisholm said.

'And why is that exactly? What have I or my clan done to you or this isle?'

'That's just it. Other than coin, your people have done nothing for any of us, despite what our family did for you.'

Confusion and frustration bubbled up in Royce again. 'What exactly have you done for us? That is what I am trying to understand. Does it have some-

thing to do with her?' He put his hand in his coat
pocket, planning to show him the brooch, but it wasn't
there. He suppressed a curse. He'd left it on the table
in Iona's cottage. Royce was certain the girl depicted
upon it was involved in the answers he sought, but
now he didn't even have it to show it to the man.

'Who?'

Royce shook his head. 'I had a miniature of a
young girl on a brooch, but in my haste to get here, I
left it behind. Just tell me what it is Webster was so
keen to hide from me that she and her sons tried to
have me killed and killed one of my best men in the
process.' He had no more time for polite conversation. He wanted answers and he wanted them now.

The older man leaned back in his chair, crossing his arms against his chest, his eyes watchful and
wary. Royce leaned forward, eager to see the change
in Chisholm's body language. He'd shifted from ag-
gressive to wary. Perhaps the girl *was* the key to everything.

'Auburn hair. Golden eyes. Distinctive looking.' He
hoped that was enough of an answer for he'd never
seen the brooch himself. He tried to remember if Iona
had used any other words to describe her childhood
friend when she'd spoken with him about it. 'She lived
here on the isle for quite some time. She was one of
your servants. Surely you remember.'

'Aye. I do remember. Catriona. She is an essential
part of it all, but only part.'

Royce longed to grab the man by the tunic and
shake him. 'Who is she?'

'Your sister.'

It was Royce's turn to lean back in shock. While Iona had told him she believed it was her friend Catriona and that there was a chance it might be a sister of his, he'd not let such an idea take root. Not really. He hadn't wanted the disappointment of being wrong, despite knowing he had at least two siblings that he remembered from his flashes of memory.

'Our sister,' a man said from behind Royce.

Our sister?

Royce turned in his chair to face the stranger.

'And who are you?' Chisholm ground out, his bushy grey eyebrows rising in scrutiny, as he stood.

'I am Rolf. Rolf Cameron. I am here for my brother.'

My brother?

Royce stood and studied the man. He filled the doorway and had a similar stature to his own. While he didn't have the scars of a warrior, he looked strong and formidable with his wild, wavy dark hair and blue eyes. His stance was wide, his hand on his waistbelt as if ready to defend. He gazed at Royce, scanning him quickly as if for injury and wellness. Upon not finding anything, his eyes softened as if in relief and Royce could see a slight tremble in the man's hand as he released his grip from his dagger handle.

'Is that the greeting I receive after searching most of the Outer Hebrides looking for you, Brother?' he scoffed, ruffling his longish and rather floppy wavy hair and half smiling at him, which made him appear a decade younger.

Royce blinked as a flash of memory seized him.

'Why do you not cut this mop of hair, Baby Brother?'
Royce teased as he stood on a stool, grabbed a matted
clump of Rolf's hair that touched his shoulders and
cut it with his blade.

His younger brother sniffed in response.

*'You must either cut it or comb it. Otherwise, this
will always happen,'* he said as he picked up another
knotted clump and sawed through it.

*Rolf whimpered as he watched his hair fall to the
floor. 'I do not feel as strong without it,'* he murmured, wiping his eyes.

*He kicked his feet back and forth in the air as he
was too young and too small for them to rest on the
floor.*

*Royce set aside his blade and knelt before his
brother. 'Your strength is in here,'* he said, setting
his index finger on the boy's chest. *'In your heart. It
will give you the will to carry on despite everything.'*

'It will?' his brother replied with another sniff.

*'Aye.' Royce smiled at him and ruffled his brother's
uneven hair with his hand.*

'Then cut it all off,' Rolf replied, lifting his chin
and pulling back his shoulders. *'I will have the heart
of a warrior instead.'*

*'Aye, my brother. You already do. You just don't
know it yet.'*

'Brother?'

Royce came back to the present and stared upon
his brother as if seeing him for the first time. Memories rushed back in quickly…too quickly. Images of
his parents, his siblings, of finding his father's jour-

nal and coming here to Lismore by boat in secret. Of Athol... The flash of his loyal friend and soldier being murdered before his very eyes crushed him. Royce gripped the chair and held on as his memories flooded back to him.

All the pain, despair and loss washed over him like a horrid wave and he felt ill. His heart and head pounded and he couldn't hear. He rushed out of the inn and stumbled into the street, gulping in fresh air. His stomach seized and he struggled, feeling along the side of the building for support. He retched once and then again.

He leaned his hands against the building, his head hanging in between, his eyes closed as he took long, steady breaths. The memories kept coming one after another until he remembered everything, even Catriona, whose real name was Violet before she was lost to their family at sea. His sister once lost and then found on this very island. The girl on the brooch. The guilt of losing her in that wave so long ago as a girl and her returning to them like a found penny almost two decades later.

He cursed.

'Good to see you, too, Brother,' Rolf said, approaching him from the street.

'I have just remembered...' Royce said with uneven breaths, 'everything.'

Rolf rested a hand on Royce's upper back. 'That is far too much for anyone. I am glad to see you, my brother. I thought you lost to the sea. We all did. And then we heard a tale of a man washed ashore with no memory and nursed to health by a sea witch.'

'What?' he asked, turning to face him, still labouring for breath.

'Susanna and I thought it just crazy enough to be true and you lucky enough to be such a man.' He gifted Royce a smile that infused him with joy and he couldn't help but smile back at his baby brother.

'I would not describe myself as lucky.'

'Then, perhaps we are the lucky ones to have you returned to us.' He let his hand fall away from Royce's back.

Or perhaps he was the lucky one.

'You have been searching for me? For how long?'

'Since the day after we realised you had left for some secret mission none of us knew of. We knew something was amiss when Athol was gone, too. Where is he?' Rolf asked. 'The man would never have left your side.'

Royce's gaze must have relayed what he couldn't bear to say aloud.

Rolf's smile flattened and he nodded. 'I expected as much but hoped for a different outcome.'

Royce stood back up and set his hands on his waist, attempting to regain his bearings.

'Do you remember what you were even doing here?' Rolf asked.

'Trying to uncover the truth of what Father did,' he replied. There was no reason to keep the secret from his siblings any more. It had almost gotten him killed.

'What do you mean?'

'There were journals I found. I thought they were only ramblings at first. You remember what Father was like at the end.' Royce walked away from the inn and stared up at the moon. Their father had been moody and confused, his mind softened by age and too much drink.

'Aye,' Rolf replied.

'But then, as I read, I realised there was something more to his stories and scattered accounts of the past. He did something.' He mustered up the courage to continue. 'He knew our youngest sister, Violet, now Catriona, was here. He chose to not bring her back to us and I wanted to know why.'

Rolf stared back blankly, his mouth dropping open in confusion. 'What?' he muttered and then his shock transformed into anger. 'All she went through could have been prevented. He left her here…on purpose?' he asked.

'Aye, and I was trying to figure out why. I hadn't wanted to tell you all in case I was wrong.'

'Well, were you wrong?'

'Nay. I am more certain than ever that some horrible secrets taint our name. And Chisholm may hold the key to getting those answers. Catriona served his family and was under his care. Now, I want to know why.'

'As do I,' Rolf growled. 'Let us go unearth the answers we seek.'

'But first…' Royce said and turned to his brother and hugged him tightly. 'Thank you for coming for me, Brother,' he said, his voice hoarse. 'Thank you.'

Rolf was stiff in Royce's hold at first, then tentatively wrapped his arms around him. Soon, he gripped him as fiercely as Royce did.

'I will always come for you,' Rolf replied. 'Just as I know you would for each one of us. We are family.'

Chapter Twenty-Three

Royce's stomach was knotted as they made their way back to The Laughing Goat Inn for more answers, his body and mind still reeling from his memories flooding back to him all at once. He walked beside his brother, his presence a welcome support as Royce's legs felt as unsteady as a new colt. Remembering everything at once, the joy, heartache and grief, and the promise of so many years, in the matter of minutes, had taken a toll on him, especially when he could remember his failings in painful and exquisite detail.

Rolf stepped into the inn and Royce fell in stride behind him. Soon, they returned to the back room where Chisholm sat as if time had stood still and they hadn't left him. The older man rolled his neck and shifted in his chair.

'Half a mind to leave, but my curiosity got the best of me,' he said.

Men like Chisholm were opportunists. Royce had known many men just like him. He could no sooner leave without finding out what he might gain as the sea could hold back the tide. Royce wasn't surprised to see him still fixed to the spot they had left him in. The old man nodded to the chairs opposite him and Royce and his brother joined him at the table.

Now that Royce's mind was full of experiences of the past and stratagem from many a battle and agreement struck, he sat quietly before he answered, weighing his options and those Chisholm would find most favourable. Coin seemed the best option, although he could think of one thing the man might want more, but Royce would hold that in reserve as a final chip in their bargaining if needed.

'Coin,' Royce said simply. 'Tell me the information I seek and coin will be provided for you. Much coin.'

Chisholm sighed. 'I have coin. Much coin. I desire something of more consequence.' He stretched his arms out on the table and laced his hands together.

So much for holding his last playing piece in reserve. 'Land,' Royce offered.

Rolf shifted in his chair. Royce could sense his brother's discomfort and he didn't blame him. If roles had been reversed, Royce would have had grave concerns about a man who'd lost his memory making agreements with a stranger over land.

'You have my interest,' the man answered. 'Where?'

'The mainland.'

'In exchange for?'

'What you know about Webster and the secret she had over our family. And what you know about Catriona. Why did she stay with you and serve under your care?'

Chisholm moved back, his cue for withdrawing a bit before deciding. A minute passed before the old man leaned forward. 'I can tell you some of it, but I don't know all. Only Webster knew the full story.' A twinge of bitterness edged into his voice and Royce filed that away for later use. Evidently, there was no love lost between him and Webster, which might work in Royce's favour.

'Then I can grant you a twenty-acre parcel of land along our eastern shore of your choosing where you can add a dock for your travels.'

'Of my choosing?'

'Aye.'

'Seems fair.'

'And I have another term.'

'Always a Cameron,' Chisholm muttered, shaking his head.

'Do not insult my family,' Rolf said, leaning forward.

'Not an insult, Son, just the truth. There is always a secondary agenda with a Cameron. You are merely fulfilling my expectation as such.'

Royce shot his brother a glance and Rolf sat back, deferring to Royce's lead.

'You will allow Miss MacKenzie to stay in her cottage. I will pay off the note due on it. I want her to own it free and clear of anyone and be allowed to reside there with her animals as long as she wishes.'

Chisholm glanced to Rolf, whose face most likely registered surprise, before he faced Royce. The old man tapped his weathered fingers on the table. 'Un-expected for a laird such as yourself.'

'I am merely repaying her for saving my life.'

Even Royce could hear the lie in his voice. He was doing it because he loved her and his heart would not allow him to do anything else. If she wouldn't come with him back to his clan, he had to know she would be protected and cared for, even if it was only by the four walls of a cottage, a rogue dog and a slew of rescue animals.

'Do you agree?' Royce demanded.

Chisholm assessed him a moment before nodding.

'Then we can proceed. Tell me what you know of your family's dealings with my own. Why were they in league with one another? And how is our youngest sister involved?'

'Bobby, bring us a round,' Chisholm called.

'Aye,' the man answered.

'One day I was at the shoreline, folding nets with Webster's father, when a man came in by boat with two other soldiers aboard. He was a fierce, imposing man and a stranger.'

'My father?' Royce asked.

'Aye. Your father.'

'What happened?'

'While I don't know what they spoke of, they shook hands at the end of it. Ever since then, your family has provided coin to us. Yearly, every May end of month like the tide coming in…until this year.'

'For how long?'

'Almost twenty years.'

'And it suddenly stopped?'

'Aye. It was one of the reasons Webster was so angry at your letters arriving with their enquiries. And then when you asked to visit…' He paused as the tankards were delivered to them. He drank some ale and wiped his mouth before continuing. 'I thought she'd choke on her own rage.'

'And why was Catriona put under your care?'

'Your father arrived but two months after the young girl was found half-dead by Nettie, the old woman who saved her and cared for her. We'd sent out word to the neighbouring clans and heard nothing. Finally, word of a child's disappearance reached us and Webster's father was a leader here at the time, so he sent a response on to your father, which precipitated his arrival that day. I believed he would claim her and bring her back home.'

'But he did not?' Rolf asked, disbelief in his voice.

'Aye. Not only did he not bring her back, but he paid our family to care for her and keep her relation to your family a secret. When old Nettie died, she was placed with what we thought would be a good family. As you now know that didn't work out, so she was put into service in the family home.'

'So, you were being paid to care for her, but also forced her to earn her keep like a servant?' Royce asked, leaning forward.

'Not I,' Chisholm answered. 'Webster's father.'

'And then you allowed her to marry that foul man, Thomas Gordon,' Rolf accused, his hair flopping down to cover part of his eyes.

'Again. Not I, but Webster's father.'

'But you did not stop it,' Royce stated.

Chisholm shifted and for the first time a bit of unease settled upon him. He didn't answer.

'But why? Why did my father not claim her and bring her back to us? It makes no bloody sense.'

'Only Webster knew.'

Royce held back the bit about the old woman alluding to one of the Cameron siblings being tainted. If Chisholm didn't know that part of the intrigue, Royce definitely wouldn't tell him. He'd be blackmailed before he could blink twice. He needed to get home and dig through Father's journals again. The answers must be there, but it would take much time to find them. And he couldn't find them here. It was time to think about heading home.

But first, he'd get the terms for the cottage settled.

'Bring me how much is owed on the note tomorrow, Chisholm. I will have funds sent to you as soon as we return home to Loch's End, along with a map to select your plot.'

'When do you plan to return home?'

'At first light.'

'Aye. I'll have one of Webster's sons drop it off for you this eve. Where will you be staying?'

'With my brother,' Royce said.

'I've a room above stairs here,' Rolf offered.

'Then I'll send it with them within the hour.' He nodded and left.

'Are you sure you wish to leave so soon?' Rolf enquired as they rose from the table.

'Aye,' Royce replied. 'I have been away too long as it is.'

'And Miss MacKenzie?' Rolf asked, raising his brows innocently, despite his enquiry being anything of the sort.

''Tis a long story, Brother.'

'Start talking, for I can't let you leave without hearing it.'

Royce smiled as they climbed the stairs to the rented room where they would share his last night in Lismore.

Chapter Twenty-Four

Iona didn't realise how much she would hate being alone again until Royce left. Mere hours had passed since his departure. After completing her chores outside, then returning inside the cottage and scrubbing everything in sight until her hands ached, she and Jack moped about the cottage as if they had never been alone before.

Finally, after she grew weary of that, she collapsed into bed. Her body ached from the strains of the day, but her mind would not allow her to sleep, nor would her heart. It ached for Royce: the feel of his calloused fingertips on her bare skin, the smell of him near and the sheer knowing he was there whether they spoke or not. She could not get him out of her mind or memory. Her body and soul yearned for him, but she also knew he would never return. Not even for the brooch he had left on the table.

Loneliness grew and filled her every thought and it was dreadful. It only reinforced her belief that she should have stayed away from him in the first place and remained alone. Jack plopped his head on her lap where she lay on the bed.

'We're being ridiculous you know,' she murmured to Jack and petted his head. 'He's just a man.' He nuzzled against her hand and sighed once more.

'Fine. Perhaps he wasn't just *any* man, but we cannot allow ourselves to be undone by it. We must get to work in finding a new place to live. We have but a week to get our situation sorted.'

Which left little time indeed. There were three widows on the island. Perhaps she could share a space with them and work to pay her share of the upkeep. While two were rather old and prone to crankiness and melancholy, there was Sorcha. She was but a few years older and had two wee ones to tend to since her husband's recent passing. The poor man had died at sea.

Iona should have gone to her to help and offer her condolences, but she never did for fear of what the woman would think of the sight of her. And what if she scared the woman's children? She shivered. She felt along the raised edges of her scar and remembered Royce's words to her.

'You describe to me places like the ruins of St Moluag and Tirefour Castle in such beauty and detail, but you do not allow yourself the pleasure of visiting them any more. All because you fear what others will think of you and your scar or do not wish to be reminded of your losses. What if no one cares about your scars, Iona? What if you walked into town and no one gave you a second glance? What if everyone

wanted to know you and you had to risk a connection with them? Would you be happy or sad?'

She released a shaky breath. What if no one cared? What if they did want to get to know her? Would she be happy or sad? It was a painful question, but perhaps he was right. Maybe some part of her allowed her scar to keep her in the cottage safe from the people of Lismore. Like the refuge of her nightly swims in the water, her cottage far removed from town was an oasis where she could survive all alone.

But what if she didn't have to be alone? What if she didn't *want* to be alone any more?

Tears welled in her eyes. She'd let Royce in and look how that had turned out. She wiped her face as the tears fell unbidden down her cheeks. Nay, she was better alone. Alone with her animals and no one else.

Royce flipped over on his side on the mattress once more and pounded the pillow before resting his head back on it. All Royce could think of was Iona and the pained look on her face when he'd last spoken to her. He had half a mind to go to her now and make amends. It didn't matter that it was the middle of the night. It didn't matter that he might be right and she was choosing such solitude as protection. He didn't want to be right. He just wanted her. And he wanted her to come with him back to Loch's End more than anything, especially now that he knew she could. He was bound to no one. They could begin a life together, if only she would risk it.

He swallowed hard. He should be focused on unearthing the truth, not Iona. His duty as laird should always come first, yet here he was, fantasising about her and what a life with her would and could be like rather than puzzling out what happened all those years ago when Catriona was deliberately left here by their father. Even now the thought of such a painful and deliberate act was hard to fathom. He wanted there to be a compelling reason for such cruelty, but he couldn't think of any reason in which a father should purposefully abandon their child. Even if she might be tainted as Webster said and not a full-blooded Cameron.

Once more Royce's mind shifted away from his duty as laird to Iona. A rogue image of what their life could have been together thrust itself to the forefront and he squeezed his eyes shut. He didn't want to imagine a life with Iona with a brood of children and rescued animals. He didn't want to imagine waking to her smooth, luscious body pressed warm to his own each morn or coupling with her each eve.

Such imaginings were a torture far too cruel for any man, no matter his crime. And he knew he had many. His memories provided him an array of personal failings, which he hoped to correct. The problem was there were too many to course correct at once. But he had decided he would focus on one first above all others to improve upon: being a better older brother to his siblings.

His body heated in embarrassment at all the memories of him keeping them at such a distance or ordering them about as if he was their father. He would work on closing the distance between them. He wanted to. Iona had taught him that family was not to be kept at arm's length, but cherished.

He knew that now.

And it wasn't too late to change it, which was its own blessing. One of many he had been given since the second chance of life he'd had after Iona pulled him from the sandy shore unconscious. He needed to make the most of that chance…with or without her by his side.

He pounded the pillow again and rolled over.

'Care to tell me what that pillow has done to deserve such treatment?' Rolf teased from the floor, followed by a loud, sleepy yawn. His brother had insisted he take the mattress although Royce should have refused; he knew he wouldn't catch a wink of sleep. Too much was on his mind and his heart.

Royce didn't answer.

'Anything to do with this sea witch you insist on paying the note on for her cottage?'

Royce thought about telling his brother to mind his own business, but he remembered his own pledge to himself but a few minutes ago: being a better brother and closing the distance between him and his siblings. The only way he could do that was if he talked to them, shared his worries and was vulnerable, even if it was awkward and embarrassing at first. He wanted to change and his first opportunity had just presented itself.

'Aye. But she is no sea witch. She is a beautiful and gifted healer.'

'And? Surely there is more to this story than two sentences.'

Royce chuckled. 'Aye. There is much more.'

'Then why are you leaving her?'

He sighed. 'It is she who will not come with me. I asked her, but she will not leave this place. She says she is needed here and cannot possibly go, but I cannot possibly stay. So, here we are.'

'Bollocks,' Rolf said.

'I couldn't agree more.'

'Would I like her?'

'She has your affinity to animals, so, yes, you would get on well. Susanna and Catriona would, too. She is strong, resilient and has so much to share with others, but she keeps herself to the far end of the island away from everyone.'

'By choice?'

'Aye. Mostly. She had an accident several years ago that scarred part of her face. She fears others will tease her and says she is better off alone.'

Rolf whistled. 'You are similar then.'

'How so?' Royce turned towards his brother, eager to know what he would say.

'This is the longest conversation we have had about anything that didn't relate to the clan's well-being. You tend to prefer to keep your own counsel.'

His words chilled Royce. It was exactly as he had feared. He had been remote just like Iona. He had chosen solitude like a turtle shell and hid within it quite successfully.

'I want to change that. Starting now. You are my brother.'

'Then we are off to a fine start.'

'What did I miss while I was away?' he asked.

'Not much,' his brother rushed out.

'Well, that sounds suspicious at best. What happened?'

'There has been some unrest along the Highlands. We continue to fortify our holdings and weaponry which is all we can do for now.'

'And?' he asked. 'Your tone relayed more news than that.'

He groaned. 'I hate secrets.'

Royce smiled. 'Only because you are poor at keeping them.'

'Catriona is with child.'

'That is glorious news!' Royce replied. Then, he paused and frowned. 'But…we cannot tell her anything about what we have discovered about Father intentionally leaving her here. We cannot risk her or her bairn's well-being. The truth would upset her.'

'Brother, there is not any way to keep this from her. You are a horrid liar and Susanna will pry it out of both of us within ten minutes of being back at Loch's End.'

Royce rested an arm over his eyes. 'You are right. We will have to find some way for the news to sound less horrific than it is or become better liars.'

Chapter Twenty-Five

Iona glanced at the brooch pinned to her simple grey gown. The familiar face of her long-lost friend Catriona smiled back at her and Iona couldn't help but smile as well. So far, the small token had done its job at providing Iona some comfort as the sun finally rose and she hoped the start of a new day would ease her longing for Royce.

Jack barked to be let back in the cottage and she opened the door. Jack rushed in. Off in the distance cresting one of the low rises along the shore, Iona saw two men walking down the beach towards the cottage, their profiles similar in size and stature. Her pulse increased and her breath hitched: one of them was Royce. She could tell by his powerful, long gait and by the way he carried himself: with purpose.

Today, his purpose seemed to be her, but she was too hurt to see him. If she saw his face and he asked her to leave with him again, she might give in and agree. And she was too scared to do anything of the sort.

She hustled back inside, removed the brooch from her dress, and stepped back out on the small woven mat outside the door, the very one she had made so Royce could know when he reached the threshold of the door and signal stepping up. Her eyes watered at the memory.

Sailor's fortune. Just leave it. Leave him. Let him go.

She set the brooch on the mat and closed the door. It was far easier said than done. She paced the floor, threatening to wear a hole through it as well as her worry stone that she clutched in her palm and rubbed with her thumb. The knock on the door shook her to her core.

Don't answer.

There was another knock.

Her hand rested on the latch, but she couldn't bring herself to lift it and open the door, so she walked back to the hearth.

'Iona?' Royce said. 'I know you are there. I saw you. Please let me come in and speak with you.'

She opened her mouth to answer, but froze and did nothing, which seemed all her body could do.

'I will speak with you here then. I am leaving today. This morn with my brother, Rolf. He came and found me just like you said he would. My memory returned when I saw him. I know everything. I am to return to our home at Loch's End in Argyll as laird. I am returning home.'

He had remembered.

She gasped and covered her mouth. His memory had returned like his sight and she could not have been happier for him. He deserved to return to his home and family as laird. He would do such good for so many people, whereas here he would just make her and Jack happy if he stayed on Lismore. Her sacrifice was necessary for the greater good.

'I still want you to come with me and share a life with me…as my wife. I love you.'

Tears welled and she walked over to the door, pressing her hand to the wood.

'I can hear you,' he said softly and she could hear the almost smile in the lilt of his voice. 'You taught me to listen to the creaks in the floorboard and to count my steps for my own safety.'

He paused and then continued. 'Thank you for saving my life, Iona MacKenzie. And for bringing me back to a place of happiness I had not had in a while. I will be indebted to you forever.'

Indebted.

As she would be to him, but still she stood, unable to move or speak.

'Thank you for the brooch,' he said. 'I remembered who the girl was and why I carried this with me when you found me. As you suspected, it is Catriona, my youngest sister. I was hoping to find answers as to why she was here before she returned to our clan. It warms my heart to know that she had you as a friend when she was here on Lismore and lost to us. She is happy now. Lives at Glenhaven with her husband and she is expecting her first bairn. And I know she will be thrilled to hear you are well.'

Iona wiped a tear from her face. Catriona was his

sister? And she was alive and well and expecting a baby? She pressed a hand to her chest. The joy and relief she felt was all consuming. Her friend was happy and she had been reunited with her family.

Indeed, miracles did happen.

'I shall tell her of you when I return,' he said. 'Perhaps you will allow her to visit you. I know she would love to see you. And perhaps, in time, you will allow me to visit, too.'

A minute of silence passed.

'Let us go, Brother,' another man said.

'Aye,' Royce replied.

Iona went to the window and watched him leave once more. And once more, he didn't turn back even though she wished for him to with all her heart.

Royce crested the hill and revelled in the sight of Loch's End. Its towering buttresses flanked the huge stone structure. Light reflected off it as if she were a gem herself and he smiled, for she was. Loch's End was a beauty and the prize of the Highlands: powerful, consuming and full of secrets. Much like Iona. His horse neighed and Royce loosened the reins and patted the stallion's neck.

Iona was a gem that he had lost his grip on. He only hoped she would be happy. The thought of her happy and safe in her cottage in Lismore would help him through the long days and endless nights without her by his side. Or at least he hoped it would.

Not too much had changed since he'd left for the remote shores of Lismore in hope of finding the answers to the many secrets scrawled in his father's journals. He wondered now if he had been a fool to seek out answers at all. What truth he had discovered was horrid and what he hadn't discovered might be worse yet.

The front doors of the castle opened as he dismounted and handed off the reins to the stable boy, who beamed up at him.

'Glad ye have returned, me laird,' he said.

Royce smiled down at him as if seeing him for the first time and maybe he was. Had he never bothered to greet the stable hands and thank them for their work? That ended today.

'Thank you, Logan. I am grateful to be home.' He ruffled the boy's hair and he giggled. The gap in his front teeth made a brief appearance as he smiled up at Royce.

Rolf walked beside him as they climbed the hill. 'Be prepared,' he said. 'Susanna has been in a state without you.'

Royce shook his head. 'No matter, Brother. I am home.'

'Brother,' Susanna said, popping her hands on her hips as she headed their way. 'We have been at our wits' end looking for you and—'

Royce scooped her up in a hug and swung her around in the air briefly before setting her down on the ground and pressing a kiss to her cheek. 'I have missed you, too, Sister.'

Susanna's wide eyes and open mouth let Royce know that he had done right by such a warm greeting.

'Is he well?' Susanna finally asked Rolf as if Royce was invisible.

'Aye. He is. May I introduce your new older brother and Laird, Royce Cameron.' He winked at them both and laughed.

'What happened to you?' she asked.

'A good knock to the head and almost drowning has put some sense in me, I suppose,' he answered. 'Thank you both for taking care of my duties while I was gone.'

Susanna's gaze went to Rolf again and he shrugged.

Royce looped his arm through hers and tugged her up against his side. 'Do not fear, Susanna. I am the same man, just a vastly improved one.'

'I do not know what to say, Brother. I cannot remember the last time you greeted me with such affection. It may take some getting used to.' She set her ice-blue eyes upon him as if he were an imposter and it cast him deeper into his purpose. He would make up for lost time and be a brother worth looking up to from now on.

It was what his siblings deserved and so did he.

Chapter Twenty-Six

A week had passed since Royce had left Lismore and Iona had applied her restless energy to a variety of tasks, most importantly finding a new home. The young widow, Sorcha, had been thrilled by Iona's proposal to move in with her at her cottage to help pay on her own note to Chisholm and to aid in caring for her little ones in exchange for a place for her and Jack to live.

She also had an interest in learning about tinctures and healing and the idea of sharing what she knew with another filled Iona with a renewed purpose. She'd even found a few farmers willing to take in the animals she would no longer be able to care for.

In truth, she had discovered all that Royce had said about her and her fears were right. Few people even noted her scar. Sorcha's children had even decided it was from a fairy's kiss and they believed she was blessed with magic.

Her heart lurched at the knowing that she could have been living more of a life for years, but her fears had kept her prisoner in her own mind, heart and cottage. Ironically, not having the cottage had freed her in a strange and unexpected way that she never could have anticipated.

Royce would not know what to make of her, to be sure.

Even now, she swam in the early morning light, undaunted by what others would think of her if they saw her along the shore. It was oddly freeing to not worry all that time about being seen or noticed. In a few more days, she would have her belongings packed and moved out of the home she had lived in for most of her life. She dunked her head and slicked back her hair before climbing out of the warm water in her shift. The blue, cloudless skies promised a lovely day and she planned on embracing it.

As she dried herself off and wrapped her cloak around her, she saw Chisholm coming down the beach. She wasn't surprised. Her two weeks would be up soon, so perhaps he was serving her a kind reminder to be out in a timely fashion. She pulled back her shoulders and lifted her chin, preparing herself for the news.

Jack rushed up to him, barking a greeting, and he petted the hound's head. She walked towards Chisholm, for there was no longer anything to be afraid of. She had already lost all she could to the man. He could take no more from her.

'Good morn, Miss MacKenzie,' he said, clutching some folded parchment and a letter in his hands. His fingertips skimmed the top of the paper over and over as he spoke.

''Tis a beautiful morn, Mr Chisholm.'

He smiled. ''Tis that.'

'What can I help you with?' she asked, squeezing excess water from her hair.

'It is I who came to help you.'

She furrowed her brow. 'I'm sorry, I don't understand.'

'Here is the deed to the cottage along with an extra key and letter.'

She pressed a finger to her ear. Perhaps water was in her ear causing her to imagine words he wasn't saying. 'I don't understand.'

'Laird Cameron and I came to a renewed agreement before he left that negates the one you and I had originally made.'

'And what is that?'

'He paid what was due on your cottage in full. You are the proud new owner. Congratulations.' He smiled and placed the deed, extra key and letter with its crested wax seal in her hands. 'I must be off,' he called and walked away as if their conversation made all the sense in the world when it made little sense at all.

What had Royce done?

She scanned the deed, which looked authentic, and then slipped it and the extra iron key in her cloak pocket. Her body shook with cold and shock. 'Let us go, Jack,' she said, jogging back up the sand and into the cottage. She would dry off, change, then read the letter.

She set it on the table and stared at her name in its swirling script on the front. Her heart clamoured irregularly in her chest. She knew it was from Royce and delayed opening it, knowing full well the contents would shred her heart and resolve to bits.

The man was undoing all the progress she had made in moving on from him in a mere sixty seconds. She yanked off her cloak and wet shift before drying her skin roughly with a towel until it was a light pink. She bound her wet hair in a knot at the nape of her neck, settled at the table with shaky hands and broke the heavy, dark wax seal with the Cameron crest pressed in it.

Iona,
It has been but a week since we parted, yet I have thought about you a thousand times each day and wondered what you were doing, saying or thinking about. I dream of your voice and miss the feel of your silky hair draped across my chest and pressing my lips upon the nape of your neck.

I miss all of you.

But I also understand why you feel you must stay on Lismore. I am sorry for what I said before I left. I want nothing more than for you to be happy and if staying on the island is the future you seek, I want to give it to you. Please accept this cottage as a small token of my gratitude for saving my life and as a sign of how much I cherished our time together and you.

> *You have taught me to be brave in an ocean*
> *of uncertainty.*
> *I love you, always,*
> *Royce*

The letter floated back to the table and she covered her eyes.

What have I done?

Royce loved her and had offered her the chance for a different life full of love, a family and adventure, yet she had cast it aside out of fear even though she also loved him. But his letter told her it wasn't too late.

Iona picked up the key on the table and rushed out the door. Jack chased her and she laughed, knowing full well that this was not a game but a chance for her to seize her future. She arrived at Sorcha's cottage out of breath, but full of hope.

'Sorcha,' she said, trying to catch her breath. 'Can you watch the cottage and the animals for me? I know it is a large request, but there is somewhere I must go and quickly.'

The young widow paused hanging her laundry on the line and her brow furrowed with concern. She rested a hand on Iona's shoulder. 'Did something happen?' she asked.

'Aye,' Iona answered, smiling. 'Something wonderful has happened and I can hardly wait to seize my future.'

Sorcha laughed and tossed her head back, her auburn curls swaying from the movement. 'Then go,' she replied. 'I can tend to the cottage and the animals, and I know my little ones would love to have Jack stay with us for a few days. Will that do?'

'That will more than do. You are an angel and you shall be rewarded for your kindness one day.' Iona knew just what she hoped that reward could be, but first she had to get to Loch's End and see Royce. She could focus on nothing else. She pressed a kiss to the woman's cheek and began the run back to her own cottage to pack. If she hoped to catch the next boat to the mainland before nightfall, she would have to hurry.

'How are you settling in, Brother?' Susanna asked.

'I am almost caught up with what I missed while I was away.' Royce set aside the clan ledgers and closed one of his father's journals which he had been reading and recording significant bits of information from to compile more clues as to why Catriona was left on Lismore and not brought back to Loch's End. Royce and Rolf had agreed to not share any information with Catriona and Susanna until they had discovered the truth. There was no need to upset them until they knew and understood the full story behind such deception and who knew how long that might take.

Susanna smiled at him and perched on the edge of the worn barn door that their father had transformed into an oversized desk for his study. 'I remember when Father used to work in here. Do you?'

'Aye. He spent most of his time chasing us out of here as he worked, or at least pretending to. More than once, Mother said he revelled in our interruptions, much like I am grateful for your interruption now.' He rubbed his eyes and yawned.

'You are much changed,' she said.

He stilled. 'How so?'

'I have not seen you so carefree since you were a child before Catriona was lost to us. The Royce of old would have barked at me for such an intrusion and sent me away, desperate to not engage with anything bordering on the personal.'

He nodded. He could remember doing that on more than one occasion and he wasn't proud of it. He leaned back in his chair. 'I am trying to be a different man. A better one.'

'I think you are.' She narrowed her gaze at him, setting those eyes upon him as if she was locking in on a rabbit about to step into a snare. 'What I want to know is who has brought about this change in you. Is it the woman Rolf mentioned? The healer?'

Royce stood and stared out the two oversized Gothic windows that allowed him to see down the glen to the loch. The bright vibrant colours of summer were much like a painting. He nested his hands in his pockets. 'Aye. She is what has changed me for the better.'

'Do you love her?'

He sighed and then answered, 'Aye.'

Susanna came around next to him and met his gaze. 'Then why did you leave her there?'

'I asked her, begged her to come back with me, but she would not. She has a life there that she is desperate to hold on to and I am a laird. I cannot abandon my people and my family and remain there.'

'And that is it? Will you give up so easily?' The challenge in her words grabbed him from his thoughts and memories of Iona.

'And what shall I do? I went to her before I left. I paid for her cottage to show my appreciation for her and sent another letter that said the same. She does not want me, Susanna. It is hard to say and acknowledge, but it is the truth.'

'Nay. She is scared, Brother. That is a much different challenge. I should know. I did the same and every day I regret not standing up to Father to be with the man I loved.'

Royce met her cool, teary gaze. The ache in her voice and the strained features of her face tugged at him.

'Jeremiah?' he asked, although he hadn't needed to.

'Aye,' she said quietly. 'And now he is gone from this world. If I could do it all again, I would have fought for him. Do not make the same mistake, Brother. Otherwise, you shall spend the rest of your days wishing for a second chance you may never have…like me.'

He reached out and squeezed her hand. She blinked back tears and let go of his hand, leaving as quietly as she had come in.

It had been over a week since he had left Lismore, but his body and mind still revolved around thoughts of and feelings for Iona. He missed everything about her and that tiny cottage on the shore. Could she even be happy here? Could they? Living alone in a cottage together was far different than being here on the mainland with the prying eyes of an entire clan upon them.

He chided himself. Such thoughts were useless things. She had made her decision to stay at Lismore and he would respect it.

Even if it broke him to bits.

Chapter Twenty-Seven

The carriage came to a rocking halt in front of the largest castle Iona had ever seen.

'Sailor's fortune,' Iona muttered, craning her neck back to take in the full scope of Loch's End. She clutched her worn satchel to her chest and stared down at her meagre gown. Why hadn't she put on her best dress before charging out to see him? She bit her lip.

'Miss?' the driver said, offering his hand to help her out. She hadn't even noticed he had opened the door.

It was now or never. She accepted his hand and stepped down on to the drive. It was too late to bolt. She had travelled all this way, so she would say her peace. If he rejected her, then at least she would know and be able to move on with her life.

The castle door opened and Iona stalled at the bottom of the stairs. A servant stepped out to greet her. Her throat dried. 'I am here to see Laird Cameron.'

'Name?'

'Iona MacKenzie.'

His eyes widened briefly and then receded. 'Come in.'

She fidgeted. 'Could you ask him to meet me out here?' she asked.

If the man thought it odd, he didn't show it, but left her at the bottom of the stairs.

Her throat dried as the minutes ticked past.

When the door finally opened and Royce appeared, emotion clogged her throat and she waved to him, unable to choke out a greeting.

He stood frozen, staring down at her. 'You are here,' he said.

'Aye,' she said, staring back at him, just as addled as he was.

He walked down each step carefully as if fearing he would startle her and cause her to bolt. Finally, he stood before her, achingly close and yet so far all in the same breath.

'You look well,' she said and meant it. He was relaxed with his tunic open at the neck and sleeves rolled up to his elbows. His hair was tousled and a bit of a beard was growing in upon his cheeks.

'And you…you look beautiful. I almost do not believe you are here before me.' He reached out a tentative hand to her cheek, letting the back of his knuckles skim delicately along her skin.

She leaned into his touch. 'I am here. And I am sorry for…everything.'

'As am I. How did you even find me?'

'I enquired about where you sailed to and Chisholm knew the area since he is to build a port here from what I hear.'

'He is.' He moved closer and a trill of anticipation travelled along her skin.

'You were right,' she blurted out. 'I was hiding from everyone in that cottage, even myself. I didn't realise it until I was forced to consider leaving it and had to reach out to others in Lismore to find a place to live. No one in town cared about my scar or my past. And I find, after living with you, I am reluctant to live alone again.' She smiled. 'So is Jack.'

'He is?'

'Aye. But not as much as I. I miss you, Royce, and I want to claim that future with you here at Loch's End, if you will have me. If you still want me, want us, that is.' She cupped his cheek.

He covered her hand with his own and closed his eyes briefly before gazing upon her. 'There is nothing more I would ever want than that. You are my purpose, Iona MacKenzie. Without you, I am lost,' he said, his voice straining with emotion.

'Then kiss me, my laird,' she said, her eyes filling with tears.

He bent down, seized her face with his hands and kissed her. Soon, the edges of her body melted into his and she couldn't tell where he began and she ended. All she knew was that in his hold was exactly where she was supposed to be.

Epilogue

One month later

The bright green leaves fluttered against the trees and Iona snuggled closer to Royce as they walked down the long stretch of meadow that linked the castle of Loch's End to the waters of Loch Linnhe. The cool breeze was a reminder that autumn was now upon them.

'How do you like your new home at Loch's End? Does it measure up to Lismore?' Royce asked.

'It is even more lovely, but only because of you, my laird,' she teased, pressing a kiss to his neck.

He wrapped an arm around her shoulder. 'Just as you make it even more lovely to me, my dear wife.'

She smiled deeply at the sound of 'wife' falling from his lips. She had never dreamed of being anyone's wife or ever having a family of her own and now both were a part of who she was and would be.

Forever.

'And your cottage on Lismore? What became of it?'

'Sorcha has settled in with her children and they

have fallen in love with the animals, as I expected they would.'

'I am pleased to hear it.'

'As am I. She is eager to continue the tradition as a healer on the island.'

Jack charged along the meadow, chasing a hare back into its burrow before releasing a disappointed yip and circling the hole.

'And Jack has settled in nicely, I think,' Iona added.

'Aye, he has. He still attempts to steal my portion of the bed each eve.'

She laughed aloud. 'Would you expect anything else?'

'Nay.'

'Shall we walk to the edge and watch the sunset?' she asked.

'Aye, but first I want to show you your wedding present.'

She baulked and turned in his arms. 'What? I thought we agreed upon no gifts?'

'We did.' He smiled wickedly. 'I meant I didn't want *you* to give *me* any gifts. You have already given me far more than a man can ask for, Iona. You have given me a second chance…at everything.' He brought her hand to his lips and brushed a kiss along her knuckles, setting a fire in her belly.

'You make it impossible to be cross with you,' she said, smiling.

'Good. I never wish for you to be so with me. Now, let us go see your surprise.' He grasped her hand and tugged her along the meadow before finally stopping before the old, abandoned barn.

'Why are we at the old barn?' she asked.

'This is to be your new refuge for any rescued animals you wish to nurse. Perhaps one day it can be a place for men and women to be nursed back to health, too.'

They continued to the barn and Royce opened the large door. 'Logan,' he called. 'Can you bring us our first rescue?'

Iona stood on her toes, eager to see within the large space that would soon be hers.

The young stable boy walked over to them carefully, running his small hand slowly over the back of the dark shiny wings of a young peregrine falcon.

'Where did you find this poor creature?' she asked the boy, running a fingertip over the bird's head.

'He was hiding in brush along the shore. Injured his wing somehow, my lady. I brought him back and asked the Laird for help.'

'It inspired me to make use of this space,' Royce offered. 'It is not used now that the newer barn and training ring built in honour of Athol has been completed south of the castle and closer to the road. Logan reminded me of what it was like to be a poor creature washed up on shore, hoping to be rescued and found by someone like you,' he said, looking at Iona.

'Well, I dare say we rescued each other, Royce.'

He smiled and ran a hand along her hair. 'Aye. We did.'

* * * * *

If you enjoyed this story
make sure to look out for the
next book in Jeanine Englert's
Secrets of Clan Cameron miniseries
coming soon!

And while you're waiting for her
next book why not check out her
Falling for a Stewart miniseries?

Eloping with the Laird
The Lost Laird from Her Past
Conveniently Wed to the Laird

Get 3 FREE REWARDS!

We'll send you 2 FREE Books plus a FREE Mystery Gift.

FREE Value Over **$20**

Both the **Harlequin® Historical** and **Harlequin® Romance** series feature compelling novels filled with emotion and simmering romance.

YES! Please send me 2 FREE novels from the Harlequin Historical or Harlequin Romance series and my FREE Mystery Gift (gift is worth about $10 retail). After receiving them, if I don't wish to receive any more books, I can return the shipping statement marked "cancel." If I don't cancel, I will receive 6 brand-new Harlequin Historical books every month and be billed just $6.19 each in the U.S. or $6.74 each in Canada, a savings of at least 11% off the cover price, or 4 brand-new Harlequin Romance Larger-Print books every month and be billed just $6.09 each in the U.S. or $6.24 each in Canada, a savings of at least 13% off the cover price. It's quite a bargain! Shipping and handling is just 50¢ per book in the U.S. and $1.25 per book in Canada.* I understand that accepting the 2 free books and gift places me under no obligation to buy anything. I can always return a shipment and cancel at any time by calling the number below. The free books and gift are mine to keep no matter what I decide.

Choose one:
☐ **Harlequin Historical**
(246/349 BPA GRNX)

☐ **Harlequin Romance Larger-Print**
(119/319 BPA GRNX)

☐ **Or Try Both!**
(246/349 & 119/319 BPA GRRD)

Name (please print)

Address _____ Apt. #

City _____ State/Province _____ Zip/Postal Code

Email: Please check this box ☐ if you would like to receive newsletters and promotional emails from Harlequin Enterprises ULC and its affiliates. You can unsubscribe anytime.

Mail to the Harlequin Reader Service:
IN U.S.A.: P.O. Box 1341, Buffalo, NY 14240-8531
IN CANADA: P.O. Box 603, Fort Erie, Ontario L2A 5X3

Want to try 2 free books from another series? Call 1-800-873-8635 or visit www.ReaderService.com.

*Terms and prices subject to change without notice. Prices do not include sales taxes, which will be charged (if applicable) based on your state or country of residence. Canadian residents will be charged applicable taxes. Offer not valid in Quebec. This offer is limited to one order per household. Books received may not be as shown. Not valid for current subscribers to the Harlequin Historical or Harlequin Romance series. All orders subject to approval. Credit or debit balances in a customer's account(s) may be offset by any other outstanding balance owed by or to the customer. Please allow 4 to 6 weeks for delivery. Offer available while quantities last.

Your Privacy—Your information is being collected by Harlequin Enterprises ULC, operating as Harlequin Reader Service. For a complete summary of the information we collect, how we use this information and to whom it is disclosed, please visit our privacy notice located at corporate.harlequin.com/privacy-notice. From time to time we may also exchange your personal information with reputable third parties. If you wish to opt out of this sharing of your personal information, please visit readerservice.com/consumerchoice or call 1-800-873-8635. **Notice to California Residents**—Under California law, you have specific rights to control and access your data. For more information on these rights and how to exercise them, visit corporate.harlequin.com/california-privacy.

HHHRLP23

Get 3 FREE REWARDS!

We'll send you 2 FREE Books plus a FREE Mystery Gift.

FREE Value Over **$20**

Both the **Harlequin® Desire** and **Harlequin Presents®** series feature compelling novels filled with passion, sensuality and intriguing scandals.

HARLEQUIN
PLUS

Try the best multimedia subscription service for romance readers like you!

Read, Watch and Play.

Experience the easiest way to get the romance content you crave.

Start your **FREE TRIAL** at
www.harlequinplus.com/freetrial.